MAUREEN CHILD

FIANCÉ IN NAME ONLY

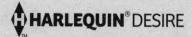

To my mom, Sallye Carberry, and my aunt, Margie Fontenot, for too many reasons to list. They are the original Matriarchs. Love you.

Recycling programs for this product may not exist in your area.

ISBN-13: 978-0-373-83875-2

Fiancé in Name Only

Copyright © 2017 by Maureen Child

Printed in U.S.A.

HARLEQUIN®
www.Harlequin.com

Maureen Child writes for the Harlequin Desire line and can't imagine a better job. A seven-time finalist for a prestigious Romance Writers of America RITA® Award, Maureen is an author of more than one hundred romance novels. Her books regularly appear on bestseller lists and have won several awards, including a Prism Award, a National Readers' Choice Award, a Colorado Romance Writers Award of Excellence and a Golden Quill Award. She is a native Californian but has recently moved to the mountains of Utah.

Books by Maureen Child

Harlequin Desire

The Fiancée Caper
After Hours with Her Ex
Triple the Fun
Double the Trouble
The Baby Inheritance
Maid Under the Mistletoe
The Tycoon's Secret Child
A Texas-Sized Secret
Little Secrets: His Unexpected Heir
Fiancé in Name Only

Pregnant by the Boss

Having Her Boss's Baby
A Baby for the Boss
Snowbound with the Boss

Visit her Author Profile page at Harlequin.com, or maureenchild.com, for more titles.

Dear Reader,

Happy 35th anniversary to Harlequin Desire! You know, there's a reason Desire is so popular. With so many wonderful writers and stories that can make you laugh or cry or both, it's no wonder that Harlequin Desire continues to shine in the publishing world! I'm so honored to work with them and here's to another thirty-five!

In *Fiancé in Name Only*, you'll meet Micah and Kelly, and hopefully, you'll love them as much as I do. Fish-out-of-water stories always appeal to me and this one is no different. Micah knows nothing about families or friends or small towns and suddenly he's learning way too much about all of them.

Kelly thinks she's happy. Content. Until Micah pulls the rug out from under her. Then she finally realizes there's more to life than being safe. These two were very hardheaded but so much fun.

I hope you enjoy this book as much as I did writing it. Visit me on Facebook and let me know what you think! And until next time, happy reading!

Maureen Child

One

"Sorry about this," Micah Hunter said. "I really liked you a lot, but you had to die."

Leaning back in his desk chair, Micah's gaze scanned the last few lines of the scene he'd just finished writing. He gave a small sigh of satisfaction at the death of one of his more memorable characters, then closed the lid of the laptop.

He'd already been working for four hours and it was past time for a break. "Problem is," he muttered, standing up and walking to the window overlooking the front of the house, "there's nowhere to go."

Idly he pulled out his cell phone, hit speed dial, then listened to the phone ring for a second or two. Finally a man came on the other line.

"How did I let you talk me into coming here for six months?"

Sam Hellman laughed. "Good to talk to you, too, man."

"Yeah." Of course his best friend was amused. Hell, if Micah wasn't the one stranded here in small-town America, he might be amused, too. As it was, though, he didn't see a damn thing funny about it. Micah pushed one hand through his hair and stared out at the so-called view. The house he was currently renting was an actual Victorian mansion set back from a wide street that was lined by gigantic, probably ancient, trees, now gold and red as their leaves changed and died. The sky was a brilliant blue, the autumn sun peeking out from behind thick white clouds. It was quiet, he thought. So quiet it was damn near creepy.

And since the suspense/horror novels Micah was known for routinely hit number one on the *New York Times* bestseller list, he knew a thing or two about *creepy.*

"Seriously, Sam, I'm stuck here for another four months because you talked me into signing the lease."

Sam laughed. "You're stuck there because you never could turn down a challenge."

Harsh but true. Nobody knew that about Micah better than Sam. They'd met when they were both kids, serving on the same US Navy ship. Sam had run away from his wealthy family's expectations, and Micah had been running from a past filled with foster homes, lies and broken promises. The two of them had connected and then stayed in touch when their enlistments were up.

Sam had returned to New York and the literary agency his grandfather had founded—discovering, after being away for a while, that he actually *wanted* to be a part of the family business. Micah had taken any construction job he could find while he spent every other waking moment working on a novel.

Even as a kid, Micah had known he wanted to write books. And when he finally started writing, it seemed the words couldn't pour out of his mind fast enough. He typed long into the night, losing himself in the story developing on the screen. Finishing that first book, he'd felt like a champion runner—exhausted, satisfied and triumphant.

He'd sent that first novel to Sam, who'd had a few million suggestions to make it even better. Nobody liked being told to change something they thought was already great, but Micah had been so determined to reach his goal, he'd made most of the changes. And the book sold almost immediately for a modest advance that Micah was more proud of than anything he'd ever earned before.

That book was the precursor of things to come. With his second book, word-of-mouth advertising made it a viral sensation and had it rocketing up the bestseller lists. Before he knew it, Micah's dreams were a reality. Sam and Micah had worked together ever since and they'd made a hell of a team. But because they were such good friends, Sam had known exactly how to set Micah up.

"This is payback because I beat you at downhill snowboarding last winter, isn't it?"

"Would I do something that petty?" Sam asked, laughter in his voice.

"Yeah, you would." Micah shook his head.

"Okay...yeah, probably," Sam agreed. "*But*, you're the one who took the bet. Live in a small town for six months."

"True." *How bad could it be?* He remembered asking himself that before signing the lease with his landlady, Kelly Flynn. Now, two months into his stay, Micah had the answer to that question.

"And, hey, research," Sam pointed out. "The book you're working on now is *set* in a small town. Good to know these things firsthand."

"Ever heard of Google?" Micah laughed. "And the book I set in Atlantis, how'd I research that one?"

"Not the point," Sam said. "The point is, Jenny and I loved that house you're in when we were there a couple years ago. And, okay, Banner's a small town, but they've got good pizza."

Micah would admit to that. He had Pizza Bowl on speed dial.

"Like I said, in another month or so, you'll feel differently," Sam said. "You'll be out enjoying all that fresh powder on the mountains and you won't mind it so much."

Micah wasn't so sure about that. But he had to admit it was a great house. He glanced around the second-floor room he'd claimed as a temporary office. The ceilings were high, the rooms were big and the view of the mountains was beautiful. The whole house had a lot of character, which he appreciated, but damned if he didn't feel like a phantom or something, wandering through the big place. He'd never had so much space all to himself and Micah could admit, at least to himself, that sometimes it creeped him out.

Hell, in the city—any city—there were lights. People. Noise. Here, the nights were darker than anything he'd ever known. Even in the navy, on board a ship, there were enough lights that the stars were muted in the night sky. But Banner, Utah, was listed on the International Dark-Sky roster because it lay just beyond a ridge that wiped out the haze of light reflection from Salt Lake City.

Here, at night, you could look up and see the Milky Way and an explosion of stars that was as beautiful as it was humbling. He'd never seen skies like these before, and he was willing to acknowledge that the beauty of it took some of the sting out of being marooned at the back end of beyond.

"How's the book coming?" Sam asked suddenly.

The change in subject threw him for a second, but Micah was grateful for the shift. "Good. Actually just killed the bakery guy."

"That's a shame. Love a good bakery guy." Sam laughed. "How'd he buy it?"

"Pretty grisly," Micah said, and began pacing the confines of his office. "The killer drowned him in the doughnut fryer vat of hot oil."

"Damn, man...that is gross." Sam took a breath and sighed it out. "You may have put me off doughnuts."

Good to know the murder he'd just written was going to hit home for people.

"Not for long, I'll bet," Micah mused.

"The copy editor will probably get sick, but your fans will love it," Sam assured him. "And speaking of fans, any of them show up in town yet?"

"Not yet, but it's only a matter of time." Frowning, he looked out the window and checked up and down the street, half expecting to see someone with a camera casing the house, hoping for a shot of him.

One of the reasons Micah never remained in one place too long was because his more devoted fans had a way of tracking him down. They would just show up at whatever hotel he was staying in, assuming he'd be happy to see them. Most were harmless, sure, but Micah knew "fan" could turn into "fanatic" in a flash.

He'd had a few talk their way into his hotel rooms, join him uninvited at dinner, acting as though they were either old friends or long-lost lovers. Thanks to social media, there was always someone reporting on where he had been seen last or where he was currently holed up. So he changed hotels after every book, always staying in big cities where he could get lost in the crowds and living in five-star hotels that promised security.

Until now, that is.

"No one's going to look for you in a tiny mountain town," Sam said.

"Yeah, that's what I thought when I was at the hotel in Switzerland," Micah reminded his friend. "Until that guy showed up determined to pummel me because his girlfriend was in love with me."

Sam laughed again and Micah just shook his head. Okay, it was funny now, but having some guy you didn't know ambush you in a hotel lobby wasn't something he wanted to repeat.

"This is probably the best thing you could have done," Sam said. "Staying in Banner and living in a house, not a hotel, will throw off the fans hunting for you."

"Yeah, well, it should. It's throwing me off, that's for sure." His scowl tightened. "It's too damn quiet here."

"Want me to send you a recording of Manhattan traffic? You could play it while you write."

"Funny," Micah said, and didn't even admit to himself that the idea wasn't half bad. "Why haven't I fired you?"

"Because I make us both a boatload of money, my friend."

Well, Sam had him there. "Right. Knew there was a reason."

"And because I'm charming, funny and about the only person in the world who's willing to put up with the crappy attitude."

Micah laughed now. He had a point. Right from the beginning, when they'd met on the aircraft carrier they'd served on, Sam had offered friendship—something Micah had rarely known. Growing up in the foster care system, moving from home to home, Micah had never stayed anywhere long enough to make friends. Which was probably a good thing since he wouldn't have been able to *keep* a friend, what with relocating all the damn time.

So he appreciated having Sam in his life—even when the man bugged the hell out of him. "That's great, thanks."

"No problem. So what do you think of your landlady?"

Frowning, Micah silently acknowledged that he was trying to *not* think about Kelly Flynn. It wasn't working, but he kept trying.

For the last two months, he'd done everything he could to keep his distance because damned if he didn't want to get closer. But he didn't need an affair. He had to live here for another four months. If he started something with Kelly, it would make things…complicated.

If it was a one-night stand, she'd get pissy and he'd have to put up with it for four more months. If it was a long-running affair, then she'd be intruding on his writing time and spinning fantasies about a future that was never going to happen. He didn't need the drama. All he wanted was the time and space to write his book so he could get out of this tiny town and back to civilization.

"Hmm," Sam mused. "Silence. That tells me plenty."

"Tells you nothing," Micah argued, attempting to convince both himself *and* Sam. "Just like there's nothing going on."

"Are you sick?"

"What?"

"I mean, come on," Sam said, and Micah could imagine him leaning back in his desk chair, propping his feet up on the corner of his desk. He probably had his chair turned toward the windows so he could look out over Manhattan.

"Hell," Sam continued, "I'm married and I noticed her. She's gorgeous, and if you tell Jenny I said that I'll deny it."

Shaking his head, Micah looked down and watched Kelly work in the yard. The woman never relaxed. She was always moving, doing something. She had ten different jobs and today, apparently, still had the time to rake up fallen leaves and bag them. As he watched, she loaded up a wheelbarrow with several bags of leaves and headed for the curb.

Her long, reddish-gold hair was pulled into a ponytail at the back of her neck. She wore a dark green sweatshirt and worn blue jeans that cupped her behind and clung to her long legs. Black gloves covered her hands, and her black boots were scarred and scuffed from years of wear.

And though she had her back to the house, he knew her face. Soft, creamy skin, sprinkled with freckles across her nose and cheeks. Grass-green eyes that crinkled at the edges when she laughed and a wide, generous mouth that made Micah wonder what she would taste like.

Micah watched her unload the bags at the curb, then wave to a neighbor across the street. He knew she'd be smiling and his brain filled with her image. Deliberately, he turned his back on the window, shut the image of Kelly out of his mind and walked back to his chair. "Yeah, she's pretty."

Sam laughed. "Feel the enthusiasm."

Oh, there was plenty of enthusiasm, Micah thought. Too much. Which was the problem. "I'm not here looking for a woman, Sam. I'm here to work."

"That's just sad."

He had to agree. "Thanks. So why'd you call me again?"

"Damn, you need to take a break. You're the one who called me, remember?"

"Right." He pushed one hand through his hair. Maybe he did need a damn break. He'd been working pretty much nonstop for the last two months. No wonder this place was starting to feel claustrophobic in spite of its size. "That's a good idea. I'll take a drive. Clear my head."

"Invite the landlady along," Sam urged. "She could show you around since I'm guessing you've hardly left that big old house since you got there."

"Good guess. But not looking for a guide, either."

"What are you looking for?"

"I'll let you know when I find it," Micah said, and hung up.

"So how's our famous writer doing?"

Kelly grinned at her neighbor. Sally Hartsfield was the nosiest human being on the face of the planet. She and her sister, Margie, were both spinsters in their nineties, and spent most of their days looking out the windows to keep an eye on what was happening in the neighborhood.

"Busy, I guess," Kelly said, with a quick glance over her shoulder at the second-story window where she'd caught a glimpse of Micah earlier. He wasn't there anymore and she felt a small twist of disappointment as she turned back to Sally. "He told me when he moved in that he would be buried in work and didn't want to be disturbed."

"Hmm." Sally's gaze flicked briefly to that window, too. "You know, that last book of his gave me nightmares. Makes you wonder how he can stand being all alone like that when he's writing such dark, scary things…"

Kelly agreed. She'd only read one of Micah's

seven books because it had scared her so badly she'd slept with a light on for two weeks. When she read a book, she wanted cheerful escape, not terror-inducing suspense. "I guess he likes it that way," she said.

"Well, everybody's different," Sally pointed out. "And I say thank goodness. Can you imagine how boring life would be if we were all the same?" She shook her head and her densely-sprayed curls never moved. "Why, there'd be nothing to talk about."

And that would be the real shame as far as Sally was concerned, Kelly knew. The woman could pry a nugget of information out of a rock.

"He is a good-looking man though, isn't he?" Sally asked, a speculative gleam in her eyes.

Good-looking? Oh, Micah Hunter was well beyond that. The picture on the back of his books showed him as dark and brooding, and that was probably done purposefully, considering what he wrote. But the man in person was so much more. His thick brown hair was perpetually rumpled, as if he'd just rolled out of bed. His eyes were the color of rich, dark coffee, and when he forgot to shave for a day or two, the stubble on his face gave him the air of a pirate.

His shoulders were broad, his hips were narrow and he was tall enough that even Kelly's own five feet, eight inches felt diminutive alongside him. He was the kind of man who walked into a room and simply took it over whether he was trying to or not.

Kelly imagined every woman who ever met him had done a little daydreaming about Micah. Even, it seemed, Sally Hartsfield, who had a grandson as old as Micah.

"He is nice looking," Kelly finally said when she noticed Sally staring at her.

The older woman sighed and fisted both hands on her hips. "Kelly Flynn, what is wrong with you? Your Sean's been gone four years. Why, if I was your age..."

Kelly stiffened at the mention of her late husband, automatically raising her defenses. Sally must have noticed her reaction because the woman stopped short, offered a smile and, thank heaven, a change of subject.

"Anyway, I hear you're showing the Polk place this afternoon to a couple coming in from California of all places."

Impressed as well as a little irked, Kelly stared at the older woman. Honestly, Kelly had only gotten this appointment to show a house the day before. "How did you know that?"

Sally waved a hand. "Oh, I have my ways."

Kelly had long suspected that her elderly neighbors had an army of spies stationed all over Banner, Utah, and this just cemented that idea. "Well, you're right, Sally, so I'd better get going. I still have to shower and change."

"Of course, dear, you go right ahead." She checked the window again and Kelly saw frustration on the woman's face when Micah didn't show up to be watched. "I've got things to do myself."

Kelly watched the woman hustle back across the street, her bright pink sneakers practically glowing against all of the fallen leaves littering the ground. The ancient oaks that lined the street stretched out gnarly branches to almost make an arbor of gold-and-red leaves hanging over the wide road.

The houses were all different, everything from small stone cottages to the dignified Victorian where Kelly had grown up. They were all at least a hundred years old, but they were well cared for and the lawns were tidy. People in Banner stayed. They were born here, grew up here and eventually married, lived and died here.

That kind of continuity always comforted Kelly. She'd lived here since she was eight and her parents were killed in a car accident. She'd moved in with her grandparents and had become the center of their world. Now, her grandfather was dead and Gran had moved to Florida, leaving the big Victorian mansion and the caretaker's cottage at the back of the property to Kelly. Since living alone in that giant house would just be silly, Kelly rented it out and lived in the smaller cottage.

In the last three years, the Victorian had rarely been empty and when it wasn't rented out by vacationers, the house and grounds had become a favorite place for weddings, big parties and even, last year, a Girl Scout cookout in the huge backyard.

And, she thought, every Halloween, she turned the front of the Victorian into a haunted house.

"Have to get busy on that," she told herself. It was already the first of October and if she didn't get started, the whole month would slip past before she knew it.

Halfway up to the house, the front door opened and Micah stepped out. Kelly's heart gave a hard thump, and down low inside her she felt heat coil and tighten. Oh, boy. It had been four long years since her husband, Sean, had died, and since then she hadn't exactly done a lot of dating. That probably explained why she continued to have this over-the-top reaction to Micah.

Probably.

He wore a black leather jacket over a black T-shirt tucked into the black jeans he seemed to favor. Black boots finished off the look of Dangerous Male and as she admired the whole package, her heartbeat thundered loud enough to echo in her ears.

"Need some help?" he asked, jerking his head toward the wheelbarrow she was still holding on to.

"What? Oh. No." *Great, Kelly. Three. Separate. Words. Care to try for a sentence?* "I mean, it's empty, so not heavy. I'm just taking it around to the back."

"Okay." He came down the wide front steps to the brick walkway lined with chrysanthemums in bright, cheerful fall colors. "I'm taking a break. Thought I'd drive around. Get my bearings."

"After two months of being in Banner?" she asked, smiling. "Yeah, maybe it's time."

His mouth worked into a partial smile. "Any suggestions on the route I should take?"

She set the wheelbarrow down, flipped her ponytail over her shoulder and thought about it. "Just about any route you take is a pretty one. But if you're looking for a destination, you could drive through the canyon down to 89. There are a lot of produce stands there. You could pick me up a few pumpkins."

He tipped his head to one side and studied her, a flicker of what might have been amusement on his face. "Did I say I was going shopping?"

"No," she said, smiling. "But you could."

He blew out a breath, looked up and down the street, then shifted his gaze back to hers. "Or, you could ride with me and pick out your own pumpkins."

"Okay."

He nodded.

"No," she said. "Wait. Maybe not."

He frowned at her.

Having an audience while she argued with herself was a little embarrassing. She could tell from his expression that Micah didn't really want her along so, naturally, she really wanted to go. Even though she shouldn't. She already had plenty to do and maybe spending time with Micah Hunter wasn't the wisest choice, since he had the unerring ability to stir her up inside. But could she really re-sist the chance to make him as uncomfortable as he made her?

"I mean, sure," she said abruptly. "I'll go, but I'd have to be back in a couple of hours. I have a house to show this afternoon."

His eyebrows arched high on his forehead. "I can guarantee you I won't be spending two hours at a pumpkin stand." He tucked his hands into the pockets of his jacket. "So? Are you coming or not?"

Her eyes met his and in those dark brown depths, Kelly read the hope she would say *no*. So, of course, she said the only thing she could.

"I guess I am."

Two

"Why are you buying pumpkins when you're growing your own?"

They were already halfway down the twisting canyon road. The mountains rose up on either side of the narrow pass. Wide stands of pine trees stood as tall and straight as soldiers, while oaks, maples and birch trees that grew within those stands splashed the dark green with wild bursts of fall color.

"And," Micah continued, "isn't there somewhere closer you could buy the damn things?"

She turned her head to look at his profile. "Sure there is, but the produce stands have the big ones."

Kelly could have sworn she actually *heard* his eyes roll. But she didn't care. It was a gorgeous fall day, she was taking a ride in a really gorgeous car—even though it was going too fast for the pass—and she was sitting beside a gorgeous man who made her nervous.

And wasn't that a surprise? Four years since her husband Sean had died and Micah was the first man to make her stomach flutter with the kind of nerves that she had suspected were dead or atrophied. The problem was, she didn't know if she was glad of the appearance of those nerves or not.

Kelly rolled down the window and let the cold fall air slap at her in lieu of a cold shower. When she got a grip, she shifted in her seat to look at Micah. "Because I grow those to give away to the kids in the neighborhood."

"And you can't keep some for yourself?"

"I could, but where's the fun in that?"

"Fun?" he repeated. "I've seen you out there weeding, clipping and whatever else it is you do to those plants. That's fun?"

"For me it is." The wind whipped her ponytail across her face and she pushed it aside to look at him. "Besides, if I was going to take lessons on fun from somebody, it wouldn't be you."

He snorted. "If you did, I'd show you more than pumpkins."

Her stomach swirled a little at the implied promise in those words, but she swallowed hard and stilled it. He was probably used to making coded statements designed to turn women into slavering puddles. So she wouldn't accommodate him. Yet.

"I'm not convinced," she said with a shrug. "You've been in town two months and you've hardly left the house."

"That's work. No time for fun."

"Just a chatterbox," she mumbled. Every word pried out of him felt like a victory.

"What?"

"Nothing," she said. "So, what's your idea of fun then?"

He took a moment to think it through, and said, "I'd start with chartering a private jet—"

"Your own personal jet," she said, stunned.

He glanced at her and shrugged. "I don't like sharing."

She laughed shortly as she thought about the last time she'd taken a flight out of Salt Lake City airport. Crowded onto a full flight, she'd sat between a talkative woman complaining about her grandchildren and a businessman whose briefcase poked her in the thigh every time he shifted in his seat. Okay, she could see where a private jet would be nice. "Well sure. Okay, your jet. Then what?"

He steered the Range Rover down the mountain road, taking the tight curves like a race-car driver. If Kelly let herself worry about it, she'd be clinging to the edges of her seat. So she didn't think about it.

"Well, it's October, so I'd go to Germany for Oktoberfest."

"Oh." That was so far out of her normal orbit she hardly knew what to say. Apparently, though, once you got Micah talking about something that interested him, he would keep going.

"It's a good place to study people."

"I bet," she murmured.

He ignored that, and said, "Writers tend to observe. Tourists. Locals. How people are interacting. Gives me ideas for the work."

"Like who to murder?"

"Among other things. I once killed a hotel manager in one of my books." He shrugged. "The guy was a jackass so, on paper at least, I got rid of him."

She stared at him. "Any plans to kill off your current landlady?"

"Not yet."

"Comforting."

"Anyway," he continued, "after a long weekend there, I'd go to England," he mused, seriously considering her question. "There's a hotel in Oxford I like."

"Not London?"

"Fewer people to recognize me in Oxford."

"That's a problem for you?" she asked.

"It can be." He took another curve that had Kelly swerving into him. He didn't seem to notice. "Thanks to social media, my fans tend to track me down. It gets annoying."

She could understand that. The photo of Micah on the back of his books was mesmerizing. She'd spent a bit of time herself studying his eyes, the way his hair tumbled over his forehead, the strong set of his jaw.

"Maybe you should take your photo off your books."

"Believe me, I've suggested it," Micah said. "The publisher won't do it."

Kelly really didn't have anything to add to the conversation. She'd never been followed by strangers desperate to be close to her and the farthest she'd ever traveled was on her last flight—to Florida to visit her grandmother. England? Germany? Not really in her lifestyle. She'd love to go to Europe. Someday. But it wouldn't be on a private jet.

She glanced out the window at the familiar landscape as it whizzed past and felt herself settle. Micah's life was so far removed from her own it made Kelly's head spin just thinking about it.

"One of these days," she said suddenly, shifting her gaze back to his profile, "I'd like to go to Scotland. See Edinburgh Castle."

"It's worth seeing," he assured her.

Of course he'd been there. Heck, he'd probably been *everywhere*. No wonder he stuck close to the house. Why would he be interested in looking around Banner, Utah? After the places he'd been, her small hometown probably appeared too boring to bother with. Well, maybe it wasn't up to the standards of Edinburgh, or Oktoberfest in Germany, but she loved it.

"Good to know," she said. "But until then, I'll plant pumpkins for the kids." She smiled to herself and let go of a twinge of envy still squeezing her insides. "I like everything about gardening. Watching the seeds sprout, then the vines spread and the pumpkins get bigger and brighter orange." Smiling, she continued. "I like how the kids on the street come by all the time, picking out the pumpkins they want, helping water, pulling weeds. They get really possessive about *their* pumpkins."

"Yeah," he said wryly. "I hear them."

He never took his eyes off the road, she noted. Was it because he was a careful driver, or was he just trying to avoid looking at her? Probably the latter. In the two months he'd been living in her Victorian, Micah Hunter had made eluding her an art form.

Sure, he was a writer, and he'd told her when he first arrived in town that he needed time alone to work. He wasn't interested in making friends, having visitors or a guided tour of her tiny town. Friendly? Not so much. Intriguing? Oh, yeah.

Could she help it if tall, dark and crabby appealed to her? Odd though, since her late husband, Sean, had been blond and blue-eyed, with an easy smile. And *nothing* about Micah was easy.

"You don't like kids?"

Briefly he slanted a look at her. "Didn't say that. Said I heard them. They're loud."

"Uh-huh," she said with a half smile. "And didn't you say last week that it was too quiet in Banner?"

His mouth tightened but, grudgingly, he nodded. "Point to you."

"Good. I like winning."

"One point doesn't mean you've won anything."

"How many points do I need then?"

A reluctant smile curved his mouth, then flashed away again. "At least eleven."

Wow. That half smile had come and gone so quickly it was like it had never been. Yet, her stomach was swirling and her mouth had gone dry. Kelly took a breath and slowly let it out again. She had to focus on what they were talking about, *not* what he was doing to her.

"Like ping-pong," she said, forcing a smile she didn't feel.

"Okay." He sounded amused.

"All right, good," Kelly said, leaning over to pat his arm mostly because she needed to convince herself she could touch him without going up in flames. But her fingers tingled, so she pulled them back fast. "Then it's one to nothing, my favor."

He shook his head. "You're actually going to keep score?"

"You started it. You gave me a point."

"Right. I'll make a note."

"No need, I'll keep track." She looked ahead because it was safer than looking at him. Then she smiled to herself. She'd gotten him to talk and had completely held her own in the conversation—until her imagination and hormones had thrown her off.

As long as she could keep those tingles and nerves in check, she could handle Mr. Magnetic.

For the next few days, Kelly was too busy to spend much time thinking about Micah. And that was just as well, she told herself. Mainly because the minute they returned from their pumpkin-shopping expedition, Micah had disappeared and she'd gotten the message.

Clearly he wanted her to know that their brief outing had been an aberration. He'd slipped back into his cave and she hadn't caught a glimpse of him since. Probably for the best, she assured herself. Easier to keep her mind on her own life, her own responsibilities if the only time she saw Micah was in her dreams.

Of course, that didn't make for restful sleeping, but she'd been tired before. One thing she hadn't experienced before were the completely over-the-top, sexy-enough-to-melt-your-brain dreams. She hated waking up hot and needy. Hated having to admit that all she really wanted to do was go back to sleep and dream again.

"And don't start thinking about those dreams or you won't get any work done at all," Kelly told herself firmly.

It wasn't hard to push Micah into the back of her mind, since she juggled so many jobs that sometimes she just ran from one to the next. Thankfully, that gave her little opportunity to sit and wonder if sex with Micah in real life would be as good as it was in her dreams.

Although if it was, she might not survive the experience.

"Still," she mused, "not a bad way to go."

She shook her head, dipped a brush into the orange tempera paint, wiped off the excess, then painted the first of an orchard of pumpkins onto the Coffee Cave's front window. Of all her different jobs, this was her favorite. Kelly loved painting holiday decorations on storefronts.

But she was also a virtual assistant, she ran websites for several local businesses, and was a Realtor who had just sold a house to that family from California. She was a gardener and landscape designer, and now she was thinking seriously about running for mayor in Banner's next election, since she was just horrified by some of the current mayor's plans for downtown. As she laid the paint out on the glass, her mind wandered.

Kelly had a business degree from Utah State, but once she'd graduated, she hadn't wanted to tie herself down to one particular job. She liked variety, liked being her own boss. When she'd decided to go into several different businesses, a couple of her friends had called her crazy. But she remembered Sean encouraging her, telling her to do whatever made her happy.

That had her pausing as thoughts of Sean drifted through her mind like a warm breeze on a cool day. A small ache settled around her heart. She still missed him even though his features were blurred in her mind now—like a watercolor painting left out in the rain.

She hated that. It felt like a betrayal of sorts, letting Sean fade. But it would have been impossible to keep living while holding on to the pain, too. Time passed whether you wanted it to or not. And you either kept up or got run over.

On that happy notion, Kelly paused long enough to look up and down Main Street. Instantly, she felt better. Banner was a beautiful little town and had been a great place to grow up. Coming here as a heartbroken eight-year-old, she'd fallen in love with the town, the woods, the rivers, the waterfalls and the people here.

Okay, Banner wasn't Edinburgh or Oxford or wherever, but it was…cozy. The buildings were mostly more than a hundred years old with creaky floors and brick walls. The sidewalks were narrow but neatly swept, and every one of the old lampposts boasted a basket of fall flowers at its base. In another month or so, there would be Christmas signs up and lights strung across the streets, and when the snow came, it would all look like a holiday painting. So, yes, she'd like to travel, see the world, but she would always come home to Banner.

Nodding to herself, she turned back to the window and quickly laid out the rest of the pumpkin patch along the bottom edge of the window.

"Well, that looks terrific already."

Kelly turned to grin at her friend. Terry Baker owned the coffee shop and made the best cinnamon rolls in the state. With short black hair, bright blue eyes and standing at about five foot two, Terry looked like an elf. Which she didn't find the least bit amusing.

The two of them had been friends since the third grade and nothing had changed over the years. Terry had been there for Kelly when Sean died. Now that Terry's military husband had deployed for the third time in four years, it was Kelly's turn to support her friend.

"Thanks, but I've got a long way to go yet," Kelly said, taking a quick look at the window and seeing a spot she'd have to fill in with a few baby pumpkins.

"Hence the latte I have brewed just for you." She held out the go-cup she carried.

"Hence?" Kelly took the coffee, savored a sip, then sighed in appreciation. "Have you been reading British mysteries again?"

"Nope." Terry stuffed her hands into her jeans pockets. "With my sad love life, I'm home every night watching the British mysteries on TV."

"Love lives can be overrated," Kelly said.

"Right." Terry nodded. "Who're you trying to convince? Me? Or you?"

"Me, obviously, since you're the only one of us with a man at the moment."

Terry leaned one shoulder against the pale rose-colored brick of her building. "I don't have one, either, trust me. It's impossible to have phone sex on an iPad when half of Jimmy's squad could walk in at any moment."

Kelly laughed, grabbed another brush and laid down a twining green vine connecting all of the pumpkins. "Okay, that would be awkward."

"Tell me about it. Remember when he called me as a surprise on my birthday and I jumped out of the shower to answer the call?" Terry shuddered dramatically. "I can still hear all the whistles from his friends who were there in the room."

Still laughing, Kelly said, "Well, that'll teach Jimmy to surprise you."

"No kidding. Now we make phone appointments." Terry grinned. "But enough about me. I hear you and the writer went for a long ride the other day."

"How did you—" Kelly stopped, blew out a breath and nodded. "Right. Sally."

"She and her sister came in for coffee yesterday and told me all about it," Terry admitted, tipping her head to one side to study her friend. "The question is, if there was something to know, why didn't I already know it?"

"Because it's nothing," Kelly said, focusing on her painting again. She added shadows and depth to the curling vines. "He took me to buy some pumpkins."

"Uh-huh. Sally says you were gone almost two hours. Either you're really picky about your pumpkins or something else was going on."

Kelly sighed. "We went for a ride."

"Uh-huh."

"I showed him around a little."

"Uh-huh."

"Nothing happened."

"Why not?"

Kelly just blinked. A couple of kids on skateboards shot down the sidewalk with a roar that startled her. "What?"

"Honey," Terry said, stepping close enough to drop one arm around Kelly's shoulders. "Sean's been gone four years. You haven't been on a single date in all that time. Now you've got this amazing-looking guy living in the Victorian for six months and you're not going to do anything about it?"

Laughing a little, Kelly shook her head again. "What should I do? Tie him up and have my way with him?"

Terry's eyes went a little dreamy. "Hmm…"

"Oh, stop it." But even as she said it, a rush of heat filled Kelly. She only enjoyed it for a second or two before tamping it right down and mentally putting out the fire.

Honestly, she didn't want or need the attraction she felt for Micah. He clearly wasn't interested and Kelly had already loved and lost. She really had zero interest in a romance. Of any kind.

"Okay, fine," Terry said, laughing. "If you're determined to shut yourself up in a closet, wrapped in wool or something, there's nothing I can do about it. But I swear, if the CIA ever needs more spies, I'm going to recommend Sally and Margie. Those two have their fingers on the pulse of everything that happens in town."

And lucky Kelly lived right across the street from them. Sean used to laugh when he saw the older ladies, noses pressed to the windows. He would sweep Kelly into an elaborate dip and kiss her senseless, saying, *"The reason they're so nosy is no one's ever kissed them senseless. So let's give them something to talk about."*

That memory brought a sad smile that she just as quickly let slide away. Remembering Sean meant not only the good times, but the pain of losing him. She'd lost enough in her life, Kelly told herself firmly.

First her parents when she was just a kid, then her grandfather, then Sean. Enough already. And the only way to ensure she never went through that kind of pain again was to never let herself get that close with anyone again.

She had Terry. Her grandmother. A couple of good friends.

Who needed a man?

Micah's image rose up in her mind and she heard a tiny voice inside her whisper, *You do. He's only here temporarily, why not take advantage? There's no future there, so no risk.*

True, Micah would only be in Banner for four more months, so it wasn't as if—no.

Don't think about it.

Sure. That would work.

"You know," Terry said, interrupting Kelly's stream of consciousness, "there's a guy in Jimmy's squad I think you'd really like…"

"Oh, no." Kelly shook her head firmly. "Don't go there, Terry. No setups. You know those never go well."

"He's a nice guy," her friend argued.

"I'm sure he's a prince," Kelly said. "But he's not *my* prince. I'm not looking for another man."

"Well, you should be." Terry folded her arms over her chest.

"Didn't you just say there was nothing you could do about it if I wanted to lock myself in a closet?"

"I hate seeing you alone all the time."

"*You're* alone," Kelly reminded her.

"For now, but Jimmy will be home in another couple of months."

"And I'm happy for you." Deliberately, Kelly turned back to her paints. She picked up the yellow and a small brush, then laid in the eyes on the first pumpkin. With the bright yellow, it would look like the pumpkin was lit by a candle. "I had a husband, Terry. Don't want another one."

From the corner of her eye, Kelly saw her friend's shoulders slump in defeat. "I didn't say I wanted you married."

"But you do."

"Not the point," Terry said stubbornly. "Sweetie, I

know losing Sean was terrible. But you're too young to live the rest of your life like a vestal virgin."

Kelly laughed. "The virgin ship sailed a long time ago."

"You know what I mean."

Of course she did. Terry had been saying pretty much the same thing for the last two years. She just didn't understand that Kelly was too determined to avoid pain to ever take the kind of risk she was talking about. Loving was great. Losing was devastating, and she'd already lost enough, thanks.

"Yeah, I do, and I appreciate the thought—"

"No, you don't," Terry said.

"You're right, I don't." Kelly glanced at her friend and smiled to take the sting out of her words. "Honestly, you're as bad as Gran."

"Oh, low blow," Terry muttered. "She's still worried?"

"Ever since Sean died and it's gotten worse in the last year or so." She focused on the paints even while she kept talking. "Gran's even started making noises about moving back here so I won't be lonely."

"Oh, man." Terry sighed. "I thought she loved living in Florida with her sister."

"She *does*." Kelly crouched down to paint in the faces of three other pumpkins. "The two of them go to bingo and take trips with their seniors club. She's having a great time, but then she starts worrying about me and—"

Her cell phone rang and Kelly stood up to drag it

from her jeans pocket. Glancing at the caller ID, she sighed and looked at Terry. "Speak of the devil…"

"Gran? Really?" Terry's eyes went dramatically wide. "Boy, her hearing's better than ever if she could catch us talking about her all the way from Florida!"

Kelly laughed. With a wince of guilt, she sent the call to voice mail.

"Seriously?" Terry sounded surprised. "You're not going to talk to her?"

"Having *one* conversation about my lack of a love life is enough for today."

"Fine." Terry held up both hands in surrender. "I'll back off. For now."

"Thanks." She tucked her phone away and tried not to feel badly about ditching her grandmother's call.

"*But,*" Terry added before she went back into the coffee shop, "just because you're not interested in a permanent man…"

Kelly looked at her.

"…doesn't mean you can't enjoy a temporary one. I'm just saying."

After she left, Kelly's brain was racing. *A temporary man.* When she went back to her painting, she was still thinking, and as an ephemeral plan began to build in her mind, a speculative smile curved her mouth.

Three

Micah hated cooking, but he'd learned a long time ago that man cannot live on takeout alone. Especially when you're in the back end of beyond and can't get anything but pizza delivered.

He took a swig of his beer and flipped cooked pasta into a skillet with some olive oil and garlic. Adding chopped tomatoes and sliced steak to the mix, he used a spatula to mix it all together. The scent was making him hungry. Most people would think it was way too early for dinner, but Micah didn't eat on a schedule.

He'd been wrapped up in his book for the last several hours, hardly noticing the time passing. As always happened, once the flow of words finally stopped, he came out of his cave like a grizzly after six months of hibernation.

"Hi."

Micah turned to look at the open back door. It was late afternoon and the cool air felt good. Of course, if he'd known he'd be invaded, Micah would have kept the door shut. Too late now, though, since there was a little boy standing there, staring at him. The kid couldn't have been more than three or four. He had light brown hair that stuck up in wild tufts all over his head. His brown eyes were wide and curious and there was mud on the knees of his jeans and the toes of his sneakers. "Who are you?"

"I'm Jacob. I live there." He waved one hand in the general direction of the house next door. "Can I go see my pumpkin?"

The sizzling skillet was the only sound in the room. Micah looked at the kid and realized that he was one of the crew who made so much noise in Kelly's garden. That still didn't explain why the kid was here, talking to Micah. "Why are you asking me?"

"Cuz Kelly's not here so I have to ask another grown-up and you're one."

Can't argue with that kind of logic. "Yeah. Sure. Go ahead."

"Okay. What're you doin'?" Jacob came closer.

"I'm cooking." Micah glanced at the boy, then, dismissing him, went back to his skillet. "Go look at your pumpkin."

"Are you hungry, too?" The boy gave him a hopeful look.

"Yeah, so you should go home," Micah told him. "Have lunch." What time was it? He looked out the window. The sky was darkening toward twilight. "Or dinner."

"I hafta see my pumpkin first and say good-night."

That was a new one for Micah. Telling a vegetable good-night. But the boy looked so…earnest. And a little pitiful in his dirty jeans with his wide brown eyes. Micah didn't do kids. Never had. Not even when he *was* a kid.

He'd kept to himself back then, too. He'd never made friends because he wouldn't have been able to keep them. Moving from home to home to home kept a foster kid wary of relationships. So he'd buried his nose in whatever books he could find and waited to turn eighteen so he could get out of the system.

But now, staring into a pair of big brown eyes, Micah felt guilt tugging at him for trying to ignore the kid. The feeling was so unusual for him he almost didn't recognize it. He also couldn't ignore it. "Fine then. Go ahead. Say good-night to your pumpkin."

"You hafta open the gate for me cuz I'm too little."

Rolling his eyes, Micah remembered the gated white-picket fence Kelly kept around her garden patch. She'd told him once it was to discourage rabbits and deer. Even though the deer could jump the fence with no problem, she wanted to make vegetable stealing as hard as possible on them.

With a sigh, Micah turned the fire off under his skillet, and said goodbye to the meal he'd just made. "All right." Micah looked at the boy. "Let's go then."

A bright smile lit the kid's face. "Thanks!"

He hustled out of the kitchen, down the back steps and around to the side of the house.

Micah followed more slowly, and as he walked, he took a second to appreciate the view. All around him fall colors exploded in shades of gold and red. The dark green of the pines in the woods beyond the house made them look as if they were made of shadows, and he idly plotted another murder, deep in the forest.

"I could have some kid find the body," he mumbled, seeing the possible scene in his mind. "Freak him out, but would he be too scared to tell anyone? Would he run for help or run home and hide?"

"Who?"

Coming back to the moment at hand, Micah looked at the child staring up at him. "What?"

"Who's gonna run home? Are they scared? Is it a boy? Cuz my brothers say boys don't get scared, only girls do."

Micah snorted. "Your brothers are wrong."

"I think so, too." Jacob nodded so hard his hair flopped across his forehead. He pushed it back with a dirty hand. "Jonah gets scared sometimes and Joshua needs a light on when he sleeps."

"Uh-huh." Way too much information, Micah

thought and wondered idly if the kid had an off switch.

"I like the dark and only get scared sometimes." Jacob shifted impatiently from foot to foot.

"That's good."

"Do you get scared?"

Frowning now, Micah watched the boy. For a second he was tempted to say no and let it drop. Then he thought better of it. "Everybody gets scared sometimes."

"Even dads?"

Micah had zero experience with fathers, but he suspected that the one thing that would terrify a man was worrying about his children. "Yeah," he said. "Even dads."

"Wow." Jacob nodded thoughtfully. "I have a rabbit I hold when I get scared. I don't think my dad has one."

"A rabbit?" Micah shook his head.

"Not a real one," Jacob assured him. "Real ones would be hard to hold."

"Sure, sure." Micah nodded sagely.

"And they poop a lot."

Micah hid the smile he felt building inside. The boy was so serious he probably wouldn't appreciate being laughed at. Did all kids talk like this? And whatever happened to not talking to strangers? Didn't people tell their kids that anymore?

"There it is," Jacob said suddenly, and pointed to the garden as he hurried to the gate and waited for Micah to open it. Once he had, Jacob raced across the uneven ground to one of the dozen or more pumpkins.

Micah followed, hands in his jeans pockets, watching the kid because he couldn't very well leave him out here alone, could he? "Which one?"

"This one." Jacob bent down to pat the saddest pumpkin Micah had ever seen.

It was smaller than the others, but that wasn't its only issue. It was also shaped like a lumpy football. It was more a pale yellow than orange, and it had what looked like a tumor growing out of one side at the top. If it had been at a store, it would have been over-looked, but here a little boy was patting it tenderly.

"Why that one?" Micah asked, actually curious about what would have made the kid pick the damn thing.

Jacob pulled a weed, then looked up at Micah. "Cuz it's the littlest one, like me." He looked at the vines and all of the other round, perfect orange blobs. "And it's all by itself over here, so it's proba-bly lonely."

"A lonely pumpkin." He wasn't sure why that statement touched him, but he couldn't deny the kid was getting to him.

"Uh-huh." Smiling again, Jacob said, "None of the other kids liked him, but I do. I'm gonna help my mom draw a happy face on him for Halloween and then he'll feel good."

The kid was worried about a pumpkin's self-esteem. Micah didn't even know what to say to that. When *he* was a kid, he'd never done Halloween. There'd been no costumes, no trick-or-treating, no carving pumpkins with his mom.

Micah had one fuzzy memory of his mother and it drifted through his mind like fog on a winter night. She was pretty—at least, he told himself that because the mental picture of her was too blurred to really tell. She had brown hair and brown eyes like his and she was kneeling on the sidewalk in front of him, smiling, though tears glittered in her eyes. Micah was about six, he guessed, a little older than Jacob. They were in New York and the street was busy with cars and people. He was hungry and cold and his mother smoothed his hair back from his forehead and whispered to him.

"You have to stay here without me, Micah."

Fear spurted inside him as he looked up at the dirty gray building behind him. The dark windows looked like blank eyes staring down at him. Worried and chewing his bottom lip, he looked back at his mother. "But I don't want to. I want to go with you."

"It's just for a little while, baby. You'll stay here where you'll be safe and I'll be back for you as soon as I can."

"I don't want to be safe, Mommy," he whispered, his voice catching, breaking as panic nearly choked him and he felt tears streaking down his face. "I want to go with you."

"You can't come with me, Micah." She kissed his

forehead, then stood up, looking down at him. She took a step back from him. "This is how it has to be and I expect you to be a good boy."

"I will be good if I can go with you," he promised. He reached for her hand, his small fingers curling around hers and holding tight, as if he could keep her there. With him.

But she only walked him up the steps, knocked on the door and gave Micah's fingers one last squeeze before pulling free. Fear nibbled at him, his tears coming faster, and he wiped them away with his jacket sleeve. "Don't leave..."

"You wait right here until they open the door, understand?"

He nodded, but he didn't understand. Not any of it. Why were they here? Why was she leaving? Why didn't she want him to be with her?

"I'll be back, Micah," she said. "Soon. I promise." Then she turned and left him.

He watched her go, hurrying down the steps, then along the sidewalk, until she was lost in the crowd. Behind him, the door opened and a lady he didn't know took Micah's hand and led him inside.

His mother never came back.

Micah shook off the memory of his first encounter with child services. It had been a long, confusing, terrifying day for him. He was sure he wouldn't be there long. His mother had said so. For the first year, he'd actually looked for her every day. After that, hope was more fragile and, finally, the hope faded completely. His mother's lies stuck with him, of course.

Hell, they still lived in a tiny, dark corner of his mind and constantly served as a reminder not to trust anyone.

But here, in Banner, those warnings were more silent than they'd ever been for him. Watching as Jacob carefully brushed dirt off his pumpkin, Micah realized that this place was like stepping into a Norman Rockwell painting. A place where kids worried about pumpkins and talked to strangers like they were best friends. It had nothing at all to do with the world that Micah knew.

And maybe that's why he felt so out of step here.

That's how Kelly found them. The boy, kneeling in the dirt, and the man standing beside him, a trapped look on his face—as if he were trying to figure out how he'd gotten there. Smiling to herself, Kelly climbed out of her truck and walked toward the garden at the side of the house. Micah spotted her first and his brown eyes locked with hers.

She felt a jolt of something hot that made her knees feel like rubber, but she kept moving. She had to admit it surprised her, seeing Micah here with Jacob. She hadn't pictured him as the kind of guy to take the time for a child. He was so closed off, so private, that seeing him now, walking through a fenced garden while a little boy talked his ears off gave her a warm feeling she couldn't quite describe.

"What're you guys up to?" she asked as she walked closer.

"I showed Micah my pumpkin," Jacob announced. "He likes mine best, he said so."

"Well, of course he did," she agreed. "Yours is terrific."

The little boy flashed Micah a wide grin. Micah, on the other hand, looked embarrassed to have been caught being nice. Interesting reaction.

"It's okay I came over, right?" Jacob asked, looking a little worried. "Micah was cooking, but he opened the gate for me and stuff."

"Sure it's okay," Kelly told him.

"Okay, I gotta go now," Jacob said suddenly, giving his pumpkin one last pat. "Bye!"

He bolted through the gate and tore across the backyard toward the house next door.

Micah watched him go. "That was fast."

Kelly laughed a little, then looked over at Micah. "You were cooking?"

He shrugged. "I was hungry."

She glanced at the lavender sky. "Early for dinner."

"Or late for lunch," he said with a shrug. "It's all about perspective."

What did it say about her that she enjoyed the sharp, nearly bitten off words he called a conversation? Kelly wondered if he'd been any easier with Jacob, but somehow she doubted it. The man might be a whiz when typing words and dialogue, but actually speaking in real life appeared to be one of his least favorite things.

"So, why keep the fence when you told me it doesn't stop the deer?

She looked around at the tall, white pickets, then walked toward the still-open gate. Micah followed her. Once through, she latched the gate after them and said, "Makes me feel better to try. Sometimes, I could swear I hear the deer laughing at my pitiful attempts to foil them."

He looked toward the woods that ran along the back of the neighborhood and stretched out for at least five miles to the base of the mountains. "I haven't seen a single deer since I've been here."

"You have to actually be outside," she pointed out.

"Right." He nodded and tucked his hands into his jeans pockets.

"There's a lot of them and they're sneaky," Kelly said, shooting a dark look at the forest. "Of course, some of them aren't. They just walk right into the garden and sneer at you."

He laughed and she looked at him, surprised. "Deer can sneer?"

"They can and do." She tipped her head to one side to stare at him. "You should laugh more often."

He frowned at that and the moment was gone, so Kelly let it go and went back to his first question. "The fence doesn't even slow them down, really. They just jump right over it." Shaking her head, she added, "They look like ballet dancers, really. Graceful, you know?"

"So why bother with the fence?"

"Because otherwise it's like I'm saying, *It's okay with me guys. Come on in and eat the vegetables.*"

"So, you're at war with deer."

"Basically, yeah." She frowned and looked to the woods. "And, so far, they're winning."

"You've got orange paint on your cheek."

"What? Oh." She reached up and scrubbed at her face.

"And white paint on your fingers."

Kelly held her hands out to see for herself, then laughed. "Yeah, I just came from a painting job and—"

"You paint, too?"

"Oh, just a little. Window decorations and stuff. I'm not an artist or anything, but—"

"Realtor, painter, website manager…" He just looked at her. "What else?"

"Oh, a few other things," she said. "I design gardens, and in the winter I plow driveways. I like variety."

His eyes flared at her admission and her stomach jumped in response. Not the kind of variety she'd meant, but now that the thought was in her brain, thank you very much, there were lots of other very interesting thoughts, too. Her skin felt heated and she was grateful for the cold breeze that swept past them.

Kelly took a deep breath, swallowed hard and said, "I should probably get home and clean up."

"How about a glass of wine first?"

Curious, she looked up at him. "Is that an invitation?"

"If it is?"

"Then I accept."

"Good." He nodded. "Come on then. We can eat, too."

"A man who cooks *and* serves wine?" She started for the back door, walking alongside Micah. "You're a rare man, Micah Hunter."

"Yeah," he murmured. "Rare."

Naturally, she was perfectly at home in the Victorian. She'd grown up there, after all. She'd done her homework at the round pedestal table while eating Gran's cookies fresh out of the oven. She'd learned to cook on the old stove and had helped Gran pick out the shiny, stainless steel French door refrigerator when the last one had finally coughed and died.

She'd painted the walls a soft gold so that even in winter it would feel warm and cozy in here, and she'd chosen the amber-streaked granite counters to complement the walls. This house was comfort. Love.

At the farmhouse sink, Kelly looked out the window at the yard, the woods and the deepening sky as she washed her hands, scrubbing every bit of the paint from her skin. Then she splashed water on her face and wiped that away, too. "Did I get it all?"

He glanced at her and nodded. "Yeah."

"Good. I like painting, but I prefer the paint on the windows rather than on me."

Kelly got the wine out of the fridge while Micah heated the pasta in the skillet. She took two glasses from a cabinet and poured wine for each of them before sitting at the round oak table watching him.

What was it, she wondered, about a man cooking that was just so sexy? Sean hadn't known how to turn the stove on, but Micah seemed confident and comfortable with a spatula in his hand. Which only made her think about what other talents he might have. Oh, boy, it had been a long time since she'd felt this heat swamping her. If Terry knew what Kelly was thinking right this minute, she would send up balloons and throw a small but tasteful party. That thought made her smile. "Smells good."

He glanced over his shoulder at her. "Pasta's easy. A few herbs, some garlic, olive oil and cheese and you're done. Plus, some sliced steak because you've gotta have meat."

"Agreed," Kelly said, taking a sip of her wine.

"Glad to hear you're not one of those *I'll just have a salad, dressing on the side* types."

"Hey, nothing wrong with a nice salad."

"As long as there's meat in it," he said, concentrating on the task at hand.

"So what made you take up cooking?"

"Self-preservation. Live alone, you learn how to cook."

Whether he knew it or not, that was an opening for questions. She didn't waste it. "Live alone, huh?"

One eyebrow lifted as he turned to look at her. "Did you notice anyone else here with me the last couple of months?"

"No," she admitted with a smile, "but you do write mysteries. You could have killed your girl-friend."

"Could have," he agreed easily. "Didn't. The only place I commit crimes is on a computer screen."

"Glad to hear it," she said, smiling. Also glad to hear he could take some teasing and give it back. But on to the real question. "So, no girlfriend or wife?"

He used the spatula to stir the pasta, then gave her a quick look. "That's a purely female question."

"Well, then, since I am definitely female, that makes sense." She propped her chin in her hand. "And it was very male of you to answer the question by not answering. Want to give it another try?"

"No."

"No you won't answer or no *is* the answer?"

Reluctantly, it seemed, his mouth curved briefly into a half smile. "I should know better than to get into a battle of words with a woman. Even being a writer, I don't stand a chance."

"Isn't that the nicest thing to say?" But she stared

at him, clearly waiting for his answer. Finally he gave her the one she was looking for.

He snorted. "No is the answer. No wife. No girl-friend. No interest."

"So you're gay," she said sagely. Oh, she knew he wasn't because the two of them had that whole hot-buzz thing going between them. But it was fun to watch his expression.

"I'm not gay."

"Are you sure?"

"Reasonably," he said wryly.

"Good to know," she said, and took a sip of wine, hiding her smile behind the rim of her glass. "I'm not, either, just so we're clear."

His gaze bored into hers and flames licked at her insides. "Also good to know."

Her throat dried up so she had another sip of wine to ease it. "How long have you been a writer?"

"A writer or a published writer?" he asked.

"There's a difference?"

He shrugged as he plated the pasta and carried them to the table. Sitting down opposite her, he took a long drink of his wine before speaking again. "I wrote stories for years that no one will ever see."

"Intriguing," she said, and wondered what those old stories would say about Micah Hunter. Would she learn more about the closed-off, secretive man by discovering who he had been years ago?

"Not very." He took a bite of pasta, "Anyway, I've been published about ten years."

"I don't read your books."

One eyebrow lifted and he smirked. "Thanks."

She grinned. "That came out wrong. Sorry. I mean, I read one of your books a few years ago and it scared me to death. So I haven't read another one."

"Then, thank you." He lifted his glass in a kind of salute to her. "Best compliment you could give me. Which book was it?"

"I don't remember the title," she said, tasting the pasta. "But it was about a woman looking for her missing sister and she finds the sister's killer, instead."

He nodded. "*Relative Danger*. That was my third book."

"First and last for me," she assured him. "I slept with the light on for two weeks."

"Thanks." He studied her. "Did you read the whole book? Or did you stop because it scared you?"

"Who stops in the middle of a book?" she demanded, outraged at the idea. "No, I read the whole thing and, terror aside, it ended well."

"Thanks again."

"You're welcome. You know, this is really good," she said, taking another bite. "Your mom teach you how to cook?"

His face went hard and tight. He lowered his gaze to his plate and muttered, "No. Learned by trial and error."

Sore spot, she told herself and changed the subject. She had secret, painful corners in her own soul, so she wouldn't poke at his. "How's your book coming? The one you're working on now, I mean."

He frowned before answering. "Slower than I'd like."

"Why?"

"You ask a lot of questions."

"The only way to get answers."

"True." He took a sip of wine. "Because the book's set in a small town and I don't know small towns."

"Hello?" Laughing, she said, "You're *in* one."

"Yeah. That's why I came here in the first place. My agent suggested it. He stayed here a couple of years ago for the skiing and thought the town would work for my research."

"*Here*, here?" she asked. "I mean, did he stay at the Victorian?"

"Yeah."

"What's his name?"

"Sam Hellman. He and his wife, Jenny, were here for a week."

"I remember them. She's very pretty and sweet and he's funny."

"That's them," Micah agreed.

Kelly took a drink of her wine. "Well, first, I'm glad your agent had a good time here. Word of mouth? Best advertising."

"For books, too," he agreed.

"But if you want to use the town for its setting and ambience, it might help if you left the house and explored a little. Get to know the place."

He ate for a couple of minutes, then finally said, "Getting out doesn't get the typing done."

Kelly shrugged and set down her glass. "But you can't get to know the town by looking through a window, either. And, if you don't know what it's like here, you've got nothing to type anyway, right?"

"I don't much like that you've got a point."

Kelly grinned. "Well, that makes two points for me, doesn't it? I'm still winning."

Unexpectedly, he laughed and the rich, warm sound seemed to ripple along her spine.

"Competitive, aren't you?"

"You have no idea," Kelly admitted. "I used to drive my grandparents crazy. I was always trying to be first in my class, or the fastest runner or—"

"Your grandparents still live here?"

"No." She picked up her wineglass and watched the light play on the golden wine. "My grandfather died six years ago and my grandmother moved to Florida to live with her sister a year later." Kelly took a sip, let the cold liquid ease her suddenly tight throat. "When my husband died four years ago, Gran came home for a few weeks to stay with me."

"You were married?" He spoke quietly, as if unsure exactly what to say.

No surprise there, Kelly thought. Most people just immediately said, *I'm sorry.* She didn't know why. Social convention? Or was it just the panic of not being able to think of anything else?

She lifted her gaze to his. "Sean died in a skiing accident."

"Must've been hard."

"Yeah," she said, nodding. "It was. And thanks for not saying you're sorry. People do, even though they have nothing to be sorry about, you know? Then I feel like I have to make them feel better, and it's just a weird situation all the way around."

"Yeah. I get that."

The expression on his face was sympathetic and that was okay. Telling someone your husband was dead was a conversation killer. "It's okay. I mean, no one ever really knows what to say, so don't worry about it." Another sip of wine to wash down the knot in her throat. "Anyway, it wasn't easy to get Gran to go back to her new life—she thought she was abandoning me. And I love that she loves me, you know? But I don't want to be a worry or a burden or a duty—not really a duty, but that little nudge of worry. I don't want to be that, either." She took a breath and smiled. "Whoa. Rambling. Anyway, Gran's still worried, and unless I can convince her I'm just fine, she's going to move back here to keep me company."

"And that's a bad thing?"

She looked at him. "Yes. It's bad. She's having a blast in Florida. She deserves to enjoy herself, not to feel like she has to move back to take care of an adult granddaughter."

Nodding, Micah leaned back in the chair, never

taking his gaze from hers. "All right. I can see that. So you know what you want. How're you going to manage it?"

Good question. There was a ridiculous idea worming its way through her mind, but it was so far out there she felt weird even entertaining the idea while Micah was here.

"I don't know yet." She smiled, had another sip of wine and said, "But, hey, as fascinating as my whirlwind life can be, enough already. I've given you my story. What's yours?"

He stiffened. "What do you mean?"

"Well, for starters," Kelly said, "have you ever been married?"

Micah shook his head. "No."

Kelly just stared at him, waiting. There had to be more than just a no.

Finally, he scowled and added, "Fine. I was engaged once."

"Engaged but not married. So what happened?"

"It didn't take." His features were tight, like the doors of a house locked against intruders.

Okay, that was obviously a dead-end subject. "You know, for a writer—someone supposedly good with words—you're not particularly chatty."

He snorted and the tension left him. "Writers *write*. Besides, men aren't 'chatty.'"

"But they do talk."

"I'm talking."

"Not saying much," she pointed out.

"Maybe there's not much to say."

"Oh, I don't believe that," Kelly told him. "There's more, you're just stingy about sharing."

He started to speak—no doubt protest, Kelly told herself, but she stopped him with another question.

"Let's try this. You're a writer and you travel all over the world, I know. But where's home?"

"Here." He studiously avoided her gaze and concentrated on the pasta.

"Yeah," she said. "For now. But before this. Where are you from?"

"Originally," he answered, "New York."

Honestly, it would probably be easier if she asked him to *write* the information and let her read it. "Okay, that's originally. How about now—and not this house."

"Everywhere," he said. "I move around."

She hadn't expected that. Everyone was from *somewhere*. "What about your family?"

"Don't have any." He stood up, took his plate to the sink, then came back for his wineglass. Lifting it for a drink, he looked at her. "And I don't talk about it, either."

Message was clear, Kelly thought. He'd put up his mental No Trespassing signs. His eyes were shuttered and his jaw was tight.

Whatever bit of closeness had opened up between them was over now. Funny that while they were talking about *her*, he was all chatty, but the minute the conversation shifted to him, he clammed up so tightly it would take a crowbar to pry words from his mouth.

It surprised her how disappointed she was about that. Since Sean died, she hadn't been as interested in a man as she was in Micah. And for a while, as they sat together sharing a meal, she'd felt that buzz humming between them like an arc of electricity. And now it was fizzling out. The expression on his face told her he was waiting for her to pry. To ask more questions. And since she hated being predictable, Kelly said simply, "Okay."

Suspicion gleamed in his eyes. "Just like that."

"Everybody's got secrets, Micah," she told him with a shrug. "You're entitled to yours." Tipping her head to one side, she asked, "Why so surprised?"

"Because most women would be hammering me with questions right now."

"Well, then, it's your lucky day, because I'm not like most women." Besides, hammering him wouldn't work.

"Got that right," he muttered.

She heard that and smiled to herself as she carried her dishes to the sink, then turned for the back door. Kelly didn't want to leave, but she knew she should. Otherwise, she might be tempted to be like every other woman in the world and try to get him to open up some more—which would be pointless and exactly what he expected.

"So, thanks for lunch or dinner or whatever. And the wine."

Micah was right behind her. "You're welcome."

His voice came from right behind her. At the open doorway, she turned and almost bumped into his chest.

"Oh, sorry." Wow, was his chest really that broad, or was she just so close it *looked* like he was taking up the whole world? Heat poured from his body, reaching for her, tingling her nerve endings. And he smelled so good, too.

Kelly shook her head, and ignored the flutter of expectation awakening in the pit of her stomach. Deliberately, she fought for lighthearted, then tipped her head back and smiled up at him. "You know, I think I should get another point."

"For what?"

"For surprising you by not asking questions." She held up three fingers and gave him a teasing smile. "So that makes it three to nothing my favor and don't you forget it."

"Not a chance in hell you would *let* me forget, is there?"

"Nope." Kelly grinned. "And how nice that you know me so well already."

"That's what I thought." He studied her as if he were trying to figure out a puzzle. But after a second or two, he nodded. "You want to keep score? Then add this into the mix."

He pulled her in close and kissed her.

Four

Everything inside Kelly lit up like a sparkler, showering her head to toe in red-hot flickers of heat and light. Instinctively, her eyes closed and her body swayed closer to him. His mouth covered hers and his arms came around her, molding her to him, and she lifted both arms to hook them around his neck.

It had been so long since she'd been kissed she was dizzy with the sensations pouring through her. God, she'd forgotten how sensations poured through her system in a kiss, the tangle of feelings that erupted. She couldn't think. Couldn't have spoken even if she had wanted to pry her mouth from his. His tongue stroked hers and the groans lifting from her throat twisted with Micah's, the soft sounds whispering into the twilight.

Breathing was becoming an issue, but she didn't care. She wanted to revel in the feeling of her body awakening as if from a coma. Fires quickened down low inside her and a tingling ache settled at her core. Need clawed at her and she moved in even closer to him. She might have stood there all night, taking what he offered, feeling her own desires tearing at her. But, as suddenly as he'd kissed her, he ended it.

Tearing his mouth from hers, he lifted his head to look down at her. From Kelly's perspective, his features were blurry. She swayed unsteadily until she slapped one hand to the door frame just for balance. As her mind defogged, her vision cleared and her heart rate dropped from racing to just really fast.

He still held her waist in a tight grip, and when he looked down into her eyes, Kelly saw that *his* eyes were a molten brown now, shot through with the fires that were burning her from the inside out.

"I think that makes it three to one now, doesn't it?" His voice was low, a deep rumble that was almost like thunder.

Points? Oh, yeah. Kelly's brain was just not working well enough at the moment to count points. But since her body was still smoldering, she had to say, "Oh, yeah. Point to you."

He gave her a slow, satisfied smile.

Reluctantly, her mouth curved, too. "You're enjoying this, aren't you?"

"I'd be a fool not to," he admitted.

"Yeah. Well." She lifted one hand to touch her fingers to her lips. "Let's not forget, I've still got three points to your one."

His smile faded and his eyes flashed as he let her go. "But the game's not over yet, is it?"

"Not even close to finished," she said, then turned and started the short walk home. She felt him watching her as she walked away and that gave her a warm rush, too. Kelly had the feeling that this game was just getting started.

She couldn't wait for round two.

Micah watched her go for ten agonizing seconds, then he shut the door firmly to keep himself from chasing after her. God, he felt like some girl-crazed teenager and that just wasn't acceptable. He was a man who demanded control. He didn't do spontaneous. Didn't veer from the plan he had for his life. And that plan did *not* include a small-town widow who tasted like a glimpse of heaven.

He wanted another taste. Wanted to feel her body pressed to his, the race of her heart, the warmth of her arms around his neck.

"Damn it." He took a deep breath to steady himself, but her scent was still clinging to him and it invaded his lungs, making itself a part of him.

His own heartbeat was a little crazed and his jeans felt like an iron cage around his hard body. Micah didn't know what had made him grab her like that. But the urge to taste her, hold her, had been too big to ignore. If he'd been thinking clearly, he never would have done it. The problem was, every time he was around Kelly, thinking was an impossible task.

"Maybe Sam's right," he told himself. "Maybe an affair is the answer." Something had to give, he thought. Because if he spent the next four months as tied up in knots as he was at the moment, he'd never get any writing done.

Something to think about.

Kelly walked home across the wide front lawn, mind racing, nerves sizzling from that unexpected but amazing kiss. She stopped halfway to the carriage house, turned around and looked at the big Victorian.

In the deepening twilight, the house looked as it had to her when she was a child—like a fairy tale. The house was painted a deep brick red with snow-white trim that seemed to define every little detail. Three chimneys jutted up from the shake roof, indicating the tiled fireplaces—in the living room, the master bedroom and the kitchen. The wide, wrap-around porch was dotted with swings, chairs and tables, inviting anyone to sit, enjoy the view and visit for a while. Double front doors were hand-carved mahogany with inset panes of etched glass. The last of the sunset glanced off the second-story windows, making them glow gold, and downstairs a lamp in the living room flashed on, telling Kelly exactly where Micah was in the house.

She lifted one hand to her mouth as she looked at that light, imagining him striding through that front door, marching across the yard to her and kissing her again. God, one kiss and all she could think was she wanted more.

"Oh, man, this could be bad…" Deliberately then, as if to prove to herself she *could*, she turned away and continued to the cottage.

It was a smaller version of the big house. Same colors, same intricate trim, made by a long-dead craftsman more than a hundred years ago. Just one bedroom, bathroom, living room and kitchen, the cottage was perfect for one person and normally, when Kelly stepped inside, it felt like a refuge.

She'd moved out of the Victorian not long after Sean's death because she simply couldn't bear the empty rooms and the echo of her own footsteps. Here, in this cottage, it was cozy and safe and, right now, almost suffocating. But that was probably because she still felt like there was a tight band around her chest.

Kelly dropped into the nearest chair and snuggled into the deep cushions. The comfort and familiarity of the cottage didn't relax her as it usually did. Shaking her head, she sighed a little and told herself to get a grip. But it wasn't easy since Micah Hunter had a real gift when it came to kissing. So, naturally, she had to wonder how gifted he was in…related areas. Oh, boy. She was in deep trouble.

The worst part was that she wanted to be in even deeper.

When her cell phone rang, she dug it out of her pocket, grateful for the distraction. Until she saw the caller ID. Guilt rose up and took another healthy bite out of Kelly's heart. She'd forgotten all about returning her grandmother's call. Seeing Micah, sharing a meal with him, had thrown her off, and then that kiss had completely sealed the deal on her mind, shutting down any thought beyond *oh, boy*!

Taking a breath, she forced a smile into her voice and answered. "Hi, Gran! I'm sorry, I just didn't have a chance to call you back before."

"That's okay, honey," her grandmother said. "I hope you were out having fun…"

Kelly sighed a little and leaned her head back against the cushioned chair. She could hear the worry in her grandmother's voice and wished she couldn't. Ever since Sean died, Gran had been worried and it didn't seem to be easing. If anything, it was getting worse. As if the older Gran got, the more she was concerned about eventually leaving Kelly on her own.

Kelly had been trying for months to convince Gran that she was fine. Happy. But nothing worked because the only thing Gran would accept was Kelly in love and married again. She wanted her settled with a family and no matter how many times

Kelly told her that she didn't need a husband, Gran remained ever hopeful.

Even knowing that Kelly had just been kissed until her brain melted wouldn't be enough to satisfy Gran. Not unless she and Micah were married or—

Suddenly, the idea she'd played with earlier came back to her. Maybe it was the kiss. Maybe it was sitting across that table from Micah, talking, laughing, sharing dinner. Whatever the reason, Kelly made a decision that she really hoped she didn't come to regret. "Actually, Gran," she said, before the still-rational corner of her brain could stop her, "I was with my fiancé."

"*What?* Oh, my goodness, that's wonderful!"

The joy in her grandmother's voice made Kelly smile and wince at the same time. Okay, yes, technically she was lying to her grandmother. But, really, she was just trying to give the older woman some peace. The chance to enjoy her life without constant worries about Kelly. That wasn't a bad thing, was it? It's not like she was pretending to be engaged for her own sake. This was completely altruistic.

"Tell me everything," Gran insisted. "Who is he? What does he do? Is he handsome?"

"It's Micah Hunter, Gran," she said, hoping a lightning bolt didn't streak out of the sky and turn her into a cinder. "The writer who's renting the Victorian for six months."

"Oh, my, a writer!"

Kelly's eyes closed tightly on another wince, but

that didn't help because Micah's image rose up in
her mind and gave her a hard look. She ignored it.

"He's very handsome and very sweet." Oh, it
was a wonder her tongue didn't simply rot and fall
out of her mouth. *Sweet?* Micah Hunter? Sexy,
yes. Prickly, oh, yeah. But she'd seen no evidence
of sweet. Still, it was something her grandmother
would want to hear. And as long as Kelly was lying
through her teeth to the woman who had raised her,
she was determined to make it a *good* lie.

"When did this happen?" Gran asked. "When
did he propose? What does your ring look like?"

Before Kelly could answer, Gran covered the
receiver and shouted, "Linda, you won't believe it!
Our girl is engaged to a writer!"

Gran's sister squealed in the background and
Kelly sighed.

"I'm putting you on speaker, sweetie. Linda
wants to hear the story, too."

Great. A command performance. Boy, it was a
good thing they didn't do video chatting.

"It just happened tonight," Kelly blurted. Her
grandmother's friends in Banner no doubt gave her
updates on Kelly, so she would know that nothing
had happened between her and Micah any sooner.

"How exciting!" Linda exclaimed, and Gran
shushed her.

"Tell us everything, honey," Gran urged. "I want
details."

"He cooked dinner tonight," Kelly continued,

and consoled herself that at least that part of the story wasn't a lie. "He proposed while we were sitting out on the porch."

"Oh, that's lovely." Gran gave a heavy sigh and Kelly felt terrible.

She was already regretting this, but she was in so deep now there was no way to back out without admitting she had lied. Nope. Couldn't do it.

"Yeah, it was lovely." Kelly nodded and kept going, making it as romantic as she could for her grandmother's sake. The woman loved watching Hallmark movies and had been known to cry at particularly touching commercials, so Kelly knew Gran would expect romance in this story.

Thinking fast, she said, "He had flowers on the porch and those little white twinkle lights hung from the ceiling. Music was playing, too," she added, telling herself to remember all of these details. "He brought out a bottle of champagne and went down on one knee and when I said yes, he kissed me."

Kissed her brainless, apparently, because otherwise why would she be inventing all of this? Oh, God, just remembering that kiss had her blood humming and heat spiraling through her body. One kiss and she was making up an engagement.

What was she doing?

"Well, good, I'm so glad to hear he gave you romance, sweetheart. I'm so happy for you." Her grandmother sniffled a little and her sister said,

"Oh, Bella, stop now. The girl's happy. You should be too."

"These are happy tears, Linda, can't you tell?"

"They're still tears, so stop it."

Kelly grimaced. Could you actually be *devoured* by guilt?

"Pay no attention to my sister," Gran said softly. "You know, honey, since you lost Sean, I've been so worried."

"I know." Kelly told herself she was doing the right thing. She was easing an old woman's heart. Making her happy. It wasn't hurting anyone. Not even Micah, really. He was only here temporarily. Heck, he didn't even have to meet her grandmother. And, when he left in four months, Kelly would simply tell Gran that they'd broken up. Maybe the very fact that Kelly had been engaged, however briefly, would be enough to assure Gran that she didn't have to worry so much.

"Will you take a picture of your ring and send it to me?"

Oops. She looked at her naked ring finger and sighed.

"Um, I don't have a ring yet," Kelly said.

"The man thought of twinkle lights but didn't bother with a ring?" Linda asked.

The two women together were really hard to stand against. "Micah wants to wait until we go to New York so we can pick one out together."

"New York?" Linda's tone changed. "How exciting!"

"Hush, Linda," Gran told her sister. "When are you going to New York, sweetie? Can you send me pictures? I'd love to show the girls at bingo."

"Sure I can, Gran." *Oh, my God, stop talking, Kelly.*

But the lies kept piling on top of each other until any second now, she'd be buried beneath a mountain of them. There was no way to stop now. She'd started all of this and she had to follow through because admitting a lie to her grandmother was simply impossible.

"I don't know when we're going to New York though..." That was true, at least. "He's busy with work and I've got Halloween coming up and—"

Gran clucked her tongue and Kelly muffled a groan.

"Well, you both just have to take the time for each other," Gran told her firmly. "Work will always be there, but this is a special time for you two."

Oh, it was special, all right. And wait until she told Micah about all of this. That scene promised to be extra special.

"Why a New York ring?" Linda demanded. "They don't sell rings in Utah?"

"Well," Kelly said, making it up as she went along, "when I told Micah I'd never been to New York, he insisted on flying me out there in a private jet so he could show me around. So, we really want to wait on the ring until then."

"Oh, my goodness," Gran whispered. "Linda, can you imagine? Private jets."

"He must be rich," Linda said thoughtfully.

"Course he is," Gran told her. "Haven't we seen his books just everywhere? Don't tell him we don't read his books because they're too scary, though, all right dear?"

"Sure, I won't tell him," Kelly promised.

"You know," Aunt Linda said, "I saw a documentary on those private jets not long ago. They've got *bedrooms* on those jets. You could live on them, I swear."

Kelly couldn't sit still anymore. She lunged out of the chair, walked to her tiny, serviceable kitchen and threw open the fridge. Grabbing the bottle of chardonnay, she pulled out the cork and took a swig straight from the bottle. Oh, if Gran could see her at that moment. Sighing a little, Kelly got a wineglass from a cabinet and poured herself what looked like eight ounces. It might not be enough.

"Well," Gran continued to argue with her sister. "They're not looking to live on the plane, for heaven's sake, and you just keep your mind out of bedrooms."

"Nothing wrong with a good romp," Linda told her sister. "It would do you good to try one."

Kelly took a big gulp of wine. She didn't want to know about her grandmother's sex life. Or her aunt's, for that matter. Actually, she didn't want to know they *had* sex lives.

"What's that supposed to mean?" Gran sounded outraged. "Just because you don't have standards…"

"I have standards," Linda countered, "but they don't get in the way of a good time."

This argument could go on all night, Kelly knew. The two women loved nothing better than arguing with each other. Drinking her wine, Kelly told herself that while they were arguing about their men friends, they weren't interrogating Kelly about *her* love life. That was something, anyway.

Halfheartedly listening to the two of them, Kelly had enough of a break from her lie fest that she had the time to start worrying about breaking all of this to Micah. How was she supposed to explain it to him when she could hardly figure out herself why she'd started all of this?

She stared out the kitchen window at the yard and the stately Victorian where the man she was using shamelessly was currently living, unaware that he'd just gotten engaged. Oh, boy.

"When's the wedding?" Linda asked suddenly.

"She's *my* granddaughter," Gran said tightly. "I'll ask the questions here. When Debbie gets engaged, then it'll be your turn. Kelly, when's the wedding, honey?"

Kelly's cousin Debbie had already insisted that she and her girlfriend were *never* getting married because the two grans would drive her insane. Kelly could understand that. After all, she'd already lived through one wedding where Gran had made and changed plans every day. If she ever really did get married again one day, she'd elope. Vegas sounded good.

But, for now, Gran was waiting for an answer and since Kelly couldn't tell the truth, she told another lie. It seemed she was on a roll.

"Oh, the wedding won't be for a while yet," she hedged, and had another drink of wine. At this rate, she was going to pass out in another few minutes. "I mean, Micah's got this book he's working on and then he has to do other writing stuff—" Oh, God, that sounded weak, even to her. What did writers have to *do*? "Um, book tours and research trips for the next book, so we probably won't be able to get married for at least another six months, maybe even a year. It all depends on Micah's work." There. That was reasonable, right?

"Wonderful," Gran said, and Kelly released a breath she hadn't realized she'd been holding. "That gives us plenty of time to *plan*. You'll have the wedding at the Victorian, of course…"

"Oh, of course," Kelly agreed, rolling her eyes so hard she heard them rattle.

"Or," Linda argued. "You could get married on the beach right here in Florida. Next summer, maybe?"

"I don't know, Aunt Linda…"

"Why would you want to get married on a beach?" Gran snorted. "All that sand in your shoes and the wind ruining your hair and seagulls poop-ing all over the place."

"It's romantic," Linda insisted.

"It's dirty," Gran countered.

"Oh, God," Kelly murmured, so quietly that the other two women on the line didn't hear her.

Completely wrapped up in their argument, the ladies didn't notice when Kelly went quiet and that was good. Carrying her wine back to the living room, Kelly dropped into a chair again and listened with only half an ear to her grandmother and aunt.

She didn't have to pay attention now. Kelly knew that she'd be hearing nothing but plans for the next four months—until Micah left and she could break this imaginary engagement. Supposing, of course, that she could talk Micah into going along with this in the first place. If she couldn't, then what? She'd have to claim insanity. That would be the only ex-cuse accepted by her family.

Guilt was becoming such a familiar companion she hardly noticed when it dropped into the pit of her stomach and sat there like a ball of ice. Wine wouldn't melt it, either, though she gave it her best shot.

Her grandmother was talking about white dresses while Linda insisted that white was outdated and Kelly wasn't a virgin, anyway.

A snort of laughter escaped her throat and Kelly was half-afraid it would turn into hysteria. Shak-ing her head, she tried to figure out the best way to approach Micah about the story she'd created. Once she hung up the phone, Gran would be calling all of her friends in Banner to share the happy news, so Micah had to be prepared for questions. And for behaving like a man in love so she could keep her grandmother blissfully unaware for four short months.

Oh, boy. Lying got out of hand so quickly Kelly could only sit and stare blankly at the wall opposite her. Really, even when a lie seemed like the best idea, it wasn't. No one ever looked far ahead as to what that lie was going to look like once other people picked it up and ran with it. But it wasn't as if she'd had a whole lot of options. She wasn't dating anyone, so she'd had to name Micah. She couldn't let her grandmother give up her new life and sacrifice herself on the altar of Sad Lonely Granddaughter.

But, even though she knew she was doing the right thing, the hole she'd dug for herself was beginning to feel like a bottomless chasm.

At least, she *hoped* it was bottomless. Otherwise, the crash landing she was going to make would be spectacular.

Micah woke up irritated. Not surprising since what little sleep he had gotten had been haunted by images of Kelly Flynn.

"Your own damn fault," he muttered. "If you hadn't kissed her…"

The taste of her was still with him. The feel of her body, warm and pliant against his. Her eager response had fired his blood to the point that it had taken everything he had just to let her go and back off.

Hell, the woman had been making him nuts for the last two months. Sexy, smart and a wiseass, Kelly was enough to bring any man to his knees.

"But damned if I will," he muttered darkly, and got out of bed. Disgusted with himself *and* her, he stalked to the bathroom, turned the water on to heat up, then stood under the shower. He let the hot water slam into his head, hoping it might wash away the last of the dreams that had tormented him and had had him waking up hard as iron.

Naturally it didn't work. It was like her features were imprinted on his brain. Her wide green eyes, the way she had lifted one hand to her lips when their kiss ended. Her smile, her ridiculous insistence on keeping track of "points" scored.

Shaking his head, he saw her in the stupid pumpkin patch talking about her war with deer, of all things. Micah had never *seen* a deer. He closed his eyes and reminded himself that he didn't want or need a woman. But maybe that was wrong, too. If he was fantasizing this much about the landlady, it had clearly been too long since he'd been with a woman.

"Gotta be it," he murmured, shutting off the water and stepping out of the tiled, glassed-in shower. "That's the reason I can't stop thinking about a woman who doesn't even know when she has orange paint on her face."

He dried off, then walked into the bedroom, not bothering to shave. Hell, he'd gotten so little sleep he'd probably slit his own throat if he attempted it.

"What I need to do is put this out of my head and get to work." Losing himself in a grisly murder was just the thing to take his mind off finding Kelly and dragging her here to his bed.

He pulled on a pair of black jeans, then tugged a forest green T-shirt over his head. Micah didn't bother with shoes. It might be gray and cold outside, but inside the old house was toasty. All he wanted was some coffee and then some quiet so he could create another murder.

As soon as he opened the bedroom door, the unmistakable scent of fresh coffee hit him hard. But it wasn't just coffee. It was bacon, too. And toast. "What kind of burglar breaks into a house to make breakfast?"

He started down the long staircase, his bare feet silent on the sapphire-blue carpet runner. Two months here and he still felt like a stranger in this big old house with its creaky doors and polished, old-world style.

He couldn't complain about anything. The house had been updated over the years and boasted comfortable furniture, every amenity and a view from every window that really was beautiful. But it was a lot more space than he was used to. A lot more quiet than he was happy with. Being solitary was part of being a writer. After all, the bottom line was sitting by yourself at a computer. If you needed people with you every damn minute, then writing was not the job for you.

But even solitary creatures needed sensory input from time to time. And being on your own in a house built for a family of a couple dozen could be a little unsettling. Hell, as a mystery/horror writer, Micah could use this house, the solitude and the woods behind the property as the perfect setting for a book.

As that thought took root in his mind, he stopped at the bottom of the stairs, considered it and muttered, "Of course I should be using this house. Why the hell aren't I?"

He continued on through to the kitchen, his senses focused on the tantalizing scents dragging him closer even while his mind figured out how big a rewrite he was looking at. To move his heroine from a small apartment in town to this big house, he'd have to change a million little things. But, he told himself, the atmosphere alone would be worth it.

A cold winter night, the heroine closed up in her bedroom, a fire burning as the wind shrieked and sleet pelted the windows. Then over that noise, she hears something else. Someone moving downstairs—when she's alone in the house.

"Oh, yeah," he told himself, nodding, "that's good. I like it."

He hit the swinging door into the kitchen, stepped inside and stopped dead. Kelly stood at the stove, stirring scrambled eggs in a skillet. Morning sunlight danced in her hair, making the red and gold shine like a new penny. Her black yoga pants clung to her behind and hugged her legs before disappearing into the tops of the black boots on her feet. She half turned toward him when he came in. Her pale green long-sleeved shirt had the top two buttons undone, giving Micah just a peek at what looked like a lacy pink bra.

Instantly his body went hard as stone again. He swallowed the groan that rose in his throat. Wasn't it enough that she'd tormented him all damn night? Why was she here first thing in the morning? Cooking? God, he needed coffee.

And the only way to get it was to deal with the woman smiling at him.

Five

"What're you doing?"

"Cooking." She smiled at him and Micah felt every drop of blood drain from his brain and head south.

After turning the fire down under the pan, she walked to the coffeemaker, poured him a cup and carried it to him.

"I made breakfast." She sounded bright, cheerful, but her eyes told a different story. There was worry there and a hesitation that put Micah on edge.

Whatever was going on, though, would be handled best *after* coffee. He took his first sip of the morning and felt every cell in his body wake up and dance. How did people survive without coffee?

After another sip or two, he felt strong enough to ask, "Why?"

"Why what?"

One eyebrow lifted. "Why are you here? Why are you cooking?"

"Just being neighborly," she said, and he didn't believe a word of it.

"Yeah." He walked to the table, sat down and had another sip. "I've been here two months. This is the first time you've been 'neighborly.'"

"Well, then, shame on me." She stirred the eggs in the pan and neatly avoided meeting his gaze. Not, Micah told himself, a good sign.

"You're not really good at prevarication."

Her eyes widened. "Oh. Good word."

"And," Micah added wryly, "not very good at stalling, either."

She sighed heavily. "Okay, yes, there is something I need to talk to you about, but after breakfast, okay?"

He grabbed a slice of bacon, took a bite and chewed. When he'd swallowed, he sent her a hard look. "There. I ate. What's going on?"

Taking a deep breath, she turned the fire off under the eggs before facing him. "I need a husband."

Not enough coffee, he told himself. Not nearly enough. But he said only, "Good luck with that."

"No," she corrected quickly. "Not a husband, really. I just need a fiancé."

"Again. Happy hunting." He got up to refill his

coffee and thought seriously about just chugging it straight from the pot.

"Micah, I need you to pretend to be my fiancé." After she blurted out that sentence, she grabbed her own cup and took a drink of coffee.

He leaned back against the granite counter, feeling the cold of the stone seep through his T-shirt and into his bones. He crossed his bare feet at the ankles, kept a tight grip on his coffee mug and looked at her. "That seems like an overreaction to one kiss."

"What?" She flushed, flipped her hair behind her shoulders and said, "For heaven's sake, this isn't about the kiss. Though, I admit, it gave me the idea…"

More confused than ever, he could only say, "What?"

"Oh, man, this is harder than I thought it would be." She dropped into a chair at the table, grabbed a slice of bacon and took a bite. "I don't even know how to say all of this without sounding crazy."

"I'll give you a clue," he said softly. "Just say it. Don't lie to me, either, trying to soften whatever it is that's going on. Just say it."

"I wasn't going to lie to you."

"Good. Let's keep it that way."

"Okay." She nodded, took another breath that lifted her breasts until he got another peek at that lacy bra, then started talking. "When I went home last night, my gran called and she started in on moving back again because I'm so alone, and before I knew what I was saying, I told her that she didn't have to worry about me being lonely anymore because I'm engaged. To *you*."

Well, he'd wanted the truth. Micah shook his head, walked to the table, sat down opposite her and waited. Objectively, as a writer, he couldn't wait to hear the rest of this story, because it promised to be a good one. As a man with zero interest in marrying *anyone*, he felt itchy enough that he snatched another piece of bacon and bit into it.

Her green eyes were flashing and her chin was up defiantly, but she chewed at her bottom lip, and that told him she was nervous. That didn't bode well.

"You have to understand, Micah. Gran's my only family and she was so sad after my grandfather passed away." She folded both hands around her coffee mug. "Then she moved to Florida with her sister, my aunt Linda, and she was happy again. Then Sean died and she came home to be with me and she started worrying and the sorrow crept back into her eyes, her voice, everything. It was like she was being *swallowed*, you know?"

No, he didn't know. He didn't have family. Didn't have the kind of deep connections she had, so he couldn't be sure if he'd have reacted the same way she did or not. But just looking at Kelly told him that she was emotionally torn in a couple of different directions.

"I finally convinced her to go back to her life by telling her I needed time alone—which wasn't a lie," she added. "And being away from here, the memories of Grandpa and Sean, helped her and she was happy again. Micah, she's determined to come back here and protect me. To sacrifice her own happiness on the altar of what she thinks of as my misery."

"*Are* you miserable?" he asked, interrupting the stream of words pouring from her.

"Of course not." She took a sip of coffee. "I mean, sure, I get lonely sometimes, but everybody does, right?"

He didn't say anything because what *could* he say? She was right. Even Micah experienced those occasional bouts when he wished there was someone there to talk to. To hold. But those moments passed, and he realized that his life was just as he wanted it.

"But when I told her I was engaged to you…" Kelly sighed helplessly. "She was so happy, Micah, that from there, I just grabbed the proverbial ball and ran with it."

"Meaning?"

"Oh." She put her head in her hands briefly, then looked up at him again. "I told her how romantic your proposal was—"

"What did I do?" Now he was just curious. He couldn't help it. This was all so far out there that it didn't even seem real. It was like watching a movie or reading a book about someone else.

Still worrying her bottom lip, she said, "You set up a candlelit dinner on the porch around back and you had roses everywhere and music playing and little twinkle lights strung over the ceiling…"

He could *see* it and thought she'd done a nice job of scene setting. "Well, I'm pretty good."

She gave a heavy sigh. "You're laughing at me."

"Trust me," he said. "Not laughing."

"Right." She nodded, swallowed hard and said, "Anyway, then you went down on one knee and asked me. But you didn't have a ring because you want to take me to New York to pick one out."

"That's thoughtful of me."

"Oh, stop." She tossed her slice of bacon onto her plate. "I feel terrible about all of this, but I was so worried that Gran was going to hop on the first plane out of Florida…" She plopped both elbows on the table and cupped her face in her palms again, making her voice sound weirdly muffled when she added, "Everything's just a mess now and if I call her back and tell her it never happened, she'll think I lied—"

"You *did* lie."

She looked up at him. "It was just a little lie."

"So now size *does* matter?" He shook his head.

"Oh, God. How can you even make jokes about this?"

"What should I do? Rant and rave? Won't change

what you told your grandmother. But I never understood," Micah said, watching her as misery crossed her face, "how people could convince themselves that *little* lies don't matter. Lies are never the answer."

"Oh." She smirked at him and Micah was pleased to see the snap and sizzle of her attitude come back. "Mr. Perfect never lies?"

"Not perfect," he told her tightly. "But, no, I don't."

"You've never had to tell a lie to protect someone you care about?"

Since he had only a handful of people he gave a flying damn about, the answer was an emphatic no. Micah didn't do lies. Hell, his mother's lie—*I'll come back for you. Soon...*—still rang in his ears. He would never do to someone what she had done to him with that one lie designed, no doubt, to make him feel better about being abandoned.

He scrubbed one hand across his face. It was too damn early to be hit with all of this and maybe that's why Micah wasn't really angry. Confused, sure. Irritated? Always. But not furious. A part of him realized he should be mad. He was used to people trying to use him to get what they wanted. It was practically expected when you were rich and famous. And those people he had no trouble getting rid of.

But Kelly was different. He looked across the table at her and noted the worry in her eyes. Why was he so reluctant to disappoint her? Why was he willing to give her the benefit of the doubt when he never did that for anyone else? She was *lying* to her grandmother. That wasn't exactly a recommendation for trustworthiness. And yet...

"Why me?" he asked abruptly. He got up, walked to the coffeepot and carried it back to the table. He filled both of their cups, then set the pot down on a folded towel. Staring at her from across the table, he said, "There have to be some local guys you could choose from. Pick someone you know. Someone who knows your grandmother and might want to help you out with this."

She took a gulp of coffee like it was medicinal brandy and she was swilling it for courage. "Why you? Who else could I tap for this? Gran knows everyone in town. She'd never believe a sudden engagement to Sam at the hardware store. Or Kevin at the diner. If anything romantic had been going on between me and someone in town, her friends would have told her about it already."

Irritating to realize she had a point.

"But you're a mystery," she continued, leaning toward him. "She knows I have a famous writer living here, but no one in town could have told her anything about you. You hardly ever leave the house, so, for all anyone knows, we could have been carrying on some torrid affair right here in the house for the last two months."

Torrid affair? Who even talked like that anymore? But as archaic as the words sounded, they were enough to make breathing a little more difficult and Micah's jeans a little tighter. Still, he shifted his mind away from what his body was feeling and forced it to focus on what she'd said.

Kelly wasn't doing this because he was rich. Or for the thrill of claiming a famous fiancé. He was her choice because no one in town knew him. Because her grandmother would believe her lie. So it wasn't *him* so much that she wanted. Probably any single renter would have done. That made him feel both better and worse.

"That's why I picked you. You're perfect."

Perfect, he thought wryly. *And handy.*

"Why should I go along with this?" Not that he was considering it, he assured himself. But he was curious what she'd come up with.

"As a favor?" she asked, throwing both hands high. "I don't know—because you're a fabulous human being and I'm flawed and you feel sorry for me?"

He snorted.

She sighed and scowled at him. "Micah, I know it's a lot. But this is really important to me. Gran's happy in Florida. She has friends, a nice life with her sister. She's enjoying herself and I don't want her to give it all up for *me*."

He heard the sincerity in her voice, read it in her eyes and knew she meant every word. And he wondered what it would be like to love someone so much you were willing to do whatever it took to make them happy? But since he avoided all closeness with everyone, he'd never know.

Hell, he'd broken off his own real engagement because, bottom line, he couldn't bring himself to trust the woman he'd proposed to. He didn't believe she loved him—because she hadn't known the *real* him. He hadn't allowed her to peek behind that curtain, so he couldn't trust that she would still care for him if she ever found out that he was a man whose past haunted every minute of his present. So he'd ended it. Walked away and vowed he'd never do that again.

Yet here he was, actually considering another engagement? This one based on a lie?

"Micah, I don't want anything from you."

He laughed shortly. "Except an engagement to fool an old woman, the lies to keep the pretense going, and a trip to New York to pick out a ring…"

"Oh, God." She flushed and shook her head. "Okay, yes, I do want you to pretend to love me. But you won't have to lie to Gran—"

"Just everyone else you know."

"Okay, yes—" She winced a little as she admitted that. "But there won't be a trip to New York and there won't be a ring, either. I can keep postponing our *trip* when I talk to Gran and—"

"More lies."

"Not more lies, just a bit more emphasis on the original lie," she argued. Frowning, she met his gaze squarely and said, "If you think I *want* to be dishonest with my grandmother, you're wrong. I love her. I'm only doing this because it's the best thing for *her*."

He drank his coffee and felt her steady gaze focus on him. As if she could will him to do this just by staring at him. And, hell, maybe it was working. He was still here and listening, right?

She must have sensed that he was weakening because she leaned toward him, elbows on the table. Did she know that the vee of her blouse gaped open wider, giving him a clear and beautiful view of the tops of her breasts?

"I'll sign anything you want, Micah," she said. "I know you probably have lots of people trying to get things from you—"

Surprised that she seemed to have picked that thought right out of his mind, he watched her carefully.

"But I'm not. Really. If you're worried I'll sue you or something, you don't have to. I don't want anything from you. Really. Just this fake engagement."

In his experience, everyone wanted something. But Micah was intrigued now. "And when I leave town? What then?"

"Then," she said, heaving a sigh as if she already dreaded it, "I'll tell Gran we broke up. She'll be upset, but this *engagement* will buy me some time. Gran will be able to stay in Florida without worrying and…" She took a breath, then lifted her coffee cup for another sip. "Maybe I'll think of a way to convince her to stay there even if I'm not engaged."

He didn't like it, but Micah couldn't see where this ploy was going to cost him anything, either. He'd only be in town four more months, and then he'd be gone and this would all be a memory. Including the fake engagement. And, he had to admit, the longer he looked at Kelly, seeing the worry in her eyes, hearing it in her voice, the more he wanted to ease it. He didn't explore the reasons he was wanting to help her out because he wasn't sure he'd like the answers.

"All right," he said, before he could think better of it.

"Whoop!" Kelly jumped out of her chair, delighted. She came around the table, bent to him and gave him a hard, quick hug. Then she stood up and smiled in relief. "That's so great. Thanks, Micah. Seriously."

That hug had sent heat shooting straight through him, so he needed a little space between him and Kelly. Fast.

"Yeah," he said, rising to put the coffeepot back on its burner. He turned around to face her. "So what do I have to do?"

"Nothing much," she assured him, and joined him at the counter, closing the distance he'd just managed to find. "Just, when we're around people in town you have to act like you're nuts about me."

"Oh." Well, he thought, that would be easy enough. Not that he was in love with her or anything. Sure, he liked her. But what he felt for her was more about extreme *lust*. So, he could sure as hell act like he *wanted* her, because he did. Now more than ever.

What he didn't want was a wife. Or a fiancée. But he'd never wanted *anything* in his life more than he wanted Kelly in bed.

She looked insulted as she stared up at him. "Oh, come on," she said. "You don't have to look so horrified about pretending to love me. It won't be that hard to do."

Hard? Not a word Micah should be thinking about at the moment. Staring into her green eyes was almost hypnotic, so Micah shifted his gaze slightly. "Yeah," he said with just a hint of sarcasm, "I think I can handle it."

She laid one hand on his arm, and once again a flash of heat shot through him. "I really appreciate this, Micah. I know it's weird, but—"

"It's okay, I get it." He didn't. Not really. How the hell could he understand real family? He'd lost whatever family he had when he was six years old. But, as a writer, he did what he always did. He put himself in someone else's point of view. Tried to look at a situation through their eyes. Over the years, he'd been in the minds of killers and victims. Children and parents.

Yet, he was coming up blank when he tried to

figure out what Kelly was thinking, feeling. In fact, she was the one woman he'd ever known who was as damn mysterious as the stories he created. Ironic, he told himself, since he made his living inventing mysteries—and now he was faced with an enigma he couldn't unravel.

It wasn't just Kelly confusing him. It was what being near her did to him that had him baffled.

And he didn't like the feeling.

A couple of hours later, Kelly was at Terry's house, wishing she was anywhere else.

"I tell you to have a steamy affair and you say no," Terry mused thoughtfully as she tapped one finger against her chin. "But you *do* get engaged. Sure that makes sense."

Kelly hung her head briefly, then lifted it to look at her best friend. Terry's place was just a block or two off Main Street. It was a small old brick house with a great backyard and what Terry called *tons of potential*. She and Jimmy were completely rehabbing the old place that Kelly had found for them, a little at a time. The living room was cozy, the kitchen was fabulous, the bathroom was gorgeous—and the rest of the house still needed work.

Sitting on her friend's couch sipping tea and eating cookies was pure comfort. Which Kelly really needed at the moment. In fact, it almost took the sting out of what Terry was saying.

"It's crazy," Kelly agreed. "I know that."

"Good for you," Terry said, injecting false cheer into her voice. "Always best to recognize when you've completely lost your mind."

"You're not helping."

"Of course I'm not helping." Terry shook her head, sending the silver hoops at her ears swinging. "For Pete's sake, Kelly, what were you thinking? You're setting yourself up for God knows what, and now there's no way out."

Kelly knew all of that, but hearing it made her feel worse somehow. Honestly, she still wasn't sure what had made her come up with this idea in the first place. And she sure didn't know why Micah had agreed.

Actually, when she'd first started talking to him that morning, she was positive he'd give her an emphatic no and tell her to get out. But the longer she talked, the more she saw him change, his features changing from irritated to sympathetic to amusement and finally acceptance. Kelly still could hardly believe he'd agreed to this, but she was super grateful he had. Yes, it was a mess, but at least for the short term, her grandmother was happy and wasn't trying to give up her own happiness for Kelly.

"You should have heard Gran though, Terry," Kelly said softly, remembering. "She was so happy when I told her Micah and I were engaged."

Terry's concerned frown only deepened. "Sure, until you 'break up.'"

Okay, yes, that conversation with her grandmother wasn't one Kelly was looking forward to. But she'd find a way to soften the disappointment. "Yeah, but until then, I've got time to think of a way to keep her from worrying."

"Well, I hope your next plan is as entertaining as this one."

Scowling, Kelly picked up a lemon cookie drizzled with thin caramel stripes and took a bite. Seriously, nobody made better cookies than Terry. People clogged up her tiny coffee shop just to buy the baked goods. And they weren't wrong to do so.

"You're my best friend," Kelly said. "You're supposed to be on my side."

"And if you wanted to rob a bank or drive off a cliff, I should just pick up my pom-poms and cheer you on?"

"That's hardly the same thing as—"

Terry held up one hand. "I'm sorry. You refused a blind date, then got engaged, instead."

"Fake engaged."

"I stand corrected." Terry finished off her tea and set the cup on the coffee table in front of them. "Really, though, I'm on your side, Kelly. I'm just not sure what your side *is*."

"If it makes you feel any better, neither am I." It had all seemed so reasonable when she'd thought of it the night before. But facing Micah with it a couple of hours ago had shaken her a little. Still, Kelly knew this was the best thing to do. The *only* thing, as far as she could tell. Gran was happy, and

Kelly didn't have to worry about the older woman giving up her new life.

Micah was fine with it—okay, maybe *fine* wasn't exactly right. *Resigned* might be better. Either way, though, Kelly was getting what she wanted: a reprieve for her worried grandmother.

As far as pretending feelings for the town's benefit, she could pretend to be in love with Micah. She would just have to keep reminding herself that it wasn't real.

Because, honestly, one kiss from that man had melted away every reservation she'd had. Every vow she'd ever made to *not* get involved with another man had simply melted under the incredible rush of heat enveloping her during that kiss. God, even remembering it could set her on fire.

So, okay, this pretense would be a little risky for Kelly. Micah Hunter was the kind of man who could slip past a woman's defenses if she wasn't careful. Even defenses as strong as hers. So Kelly would be *very* careful.

She popped the last of the cookie into her mouth, then said, "Okay, enough 'torture Kelly' time."

"Oh, I'm not nearly finished," Terry told her.

"Fine. We'll pick it up again later, but, for now, are you going to help me with the load of plywood I need to pick up or not?"

"Sure." Terry shrugged and pushed off the couch. "Get engaged, then build a haunted house. What could be more normal?"

Kelly reached for another cookie as Terry picked up the plate and cups to take back to the kitchen. Sighing, Terry said, "And I bet you want to take some cookies home with you."

"That'd be great," Kelly said. "Thank you, very-best-friend-in-the-world-who-is-always-on-my-side-and-only-wants-what's-best-for-me."

Laughing, Terry shook her head and said, "I'll put some in a bag for you."

Kelly grinned as she tugged on her sweatshirt. "Thanks. And to respond to your earlier statement...*normal* is way overrated."

But, while she waited for Terry, Kelly's smile faded and her brain raced. Images of Micah rose up in her mind, and instantly a curl of something dangerous spun in the pit of her stomach.

Yeah. Maybe this fake engagement wasn't such a great idea, after all.

Six

Micah came out of the house as soon as he saw the two women struggling to pull sheets of plywood out of the back of Kelly's truck.

"So much for getting any work done," he muttered, and made a mental note to tell Sam that if this book went in late, it would be *his* fault. How the hell was Micah supposed to get work done when Kelly was always interrupting? Even when she wasn't there, thoughts of her plagued him, interfering with his concentration and leaving him staring into space as he willed his body into submission.

Hell, how did *any* writer work when they had people coming in and out of their lives? There was just no way to concentrate on your fictional world when the *real* world kept intruding.

As he approached, he noticed for the first time that Kelly's truck had definitely seen better days. It had once been red, but now was an oxidized sickly pink. There were rust spots along the bottom of the body, no doubt caused by all the salt used on winter roads to prevent skidding. There was an old dent in the back right fender, and he had a feeling the inside of the damn thing was no prettier than the outside.

Frowning, he remembered that Kelly had said she plowed driveways and roads during the winter. Did she use this truck? Of course she did, and it probably hadn't even occurred to her that it looked as if it was on its last legs. He didn't like the idea of her out in some snowstorm in a broken-down truck, freezing to death in the cab while she waited for someone to dig her out of a snowdrift—and, yeah, sometimes being a writer was a bad thing. His mind was all too willing to make up the worst-possible scenario of any given situation just to torture him. He shook off the vague ideas and focused on the now.

He was down the front steps and headed across the lawn before either woman noticed him. Kelly had her back to him, but the tiny woman with dark hair and wide silver hoops at her ears spotted him.

Tipping her head back, she stared at the gray sky and shouted to whoever might be listening, "Thank you!"

Looking back at Micah, she grinned. "Well, hi,

gorgeous. You must be the new fiancé. I'm the best friend, Terry."

"Good to meet you." It was impossible to *not* smile back at a woman who looked like a seductive elf. "I'm Micah."

Kelly jolted upright from where she was bent over trying to lift one end of the boards. Seductive elf or not, the only woman Micah could see was Kelly. Her hair was back in a ponytail, her gray sweatshirt was paint stained, and her worn denim jeans were ripped high on her right thigh. She must have changed into work clothes after she'd left him that morning. And even in what she was wearing right now, she looked amazing.

She dropped the plywood sheets she was trying to maneuver, and they clattered when they hit the truck bed. Straightening up, she smiled a little nervously. "Um, hi, Micah. This is Terry."

"Yeah, we met." He walked closer, looked into the truck bed, then up at Kelly. "What's all this for?"

She pushed one stray windblown lock of hair out of her face. "Every year I build a haunted house for the kids."

That didn't even surprise him. "Of course you do."

Kelly kept talking. "Last year Terry's husband, Jimmy, helped me out, but he's deployed this year."

Terry sat on the edge of the truck. "I think Kelly misses him almost as much as I do."

* * *

"Today I do," Kelly agreed. Her heart flipped over as Micah's gaze was fixed on her with the wariness of a man waiting to see if a suspicious package will explode. And of course she *had* to look absolutely hideous. "So, Micah, can you help carry these boards to the front of the house?"

"I can." He dropped both hands onto the side of the truck. "Does it get me a point?"

"A what?" Terry asked.

"No," Kelly said, smiling because he was acting as he always had around her. Things weren't awkward and she'd worried about that. Oh, she knew he was as good as his word and that he'd act like her lover in public. But she'd been afraid that asking him to do this for her might make things weird between them in private. "This is a favor. Not a point earner."

"What points are we talking about?" Terry looked from one to the other of them.

"Hmm," he mused, "seems to me I already did you a favor earlier. If I do this one, as well, that's two in one day. Is there any kind of payoff for a favor?"

"What'd you have in mind?" Kelly's stomach did a fast spin and roll. Honestly, the man's eyes were so dark that when they were fastened on her, as they were now, she could feel the earth beneath her feet slide and shift.

"Another kiss," he said.

All of her breath left her in a rush.

"Okay," Terry murmured. "This is getting interesting. Wait a minute. Did he say *another* kiss?"

Kelly paid no attention to Terry because she couldn't see anything but Micah. It took everything in Kelly not to vault over the side of the truck and lock her mouth onto his. Just the thought of being held close to him again made her want it more than anything. But she had a question first. "Why?"

He shrugged and his broad chest sort of rippled beneath his black T-shirt. "You said we needed to put on a show in front of people, right?"

"Yeah…" she said, "but Terry doesn't count."

"Thanks very much," Terry said, "however, since Jimmy's gone, I wouldn't mind seeing a red-hot kiss. A little vicarious living would do me worlds of good."

"Pay no attention to her," Kelly advised.

"I wasn't talking about Terry," Micah said, his gaze flicking briefly to a point over Kelly's shoulder. "I was talking about the two old women watching from their window."

"Oh, God…" Kelly murmured. She'd forgotten all about her neighbors, but the two sisters probably had their noses pressed to the glass.

"Hi!" Terry shouted as she turned to wave at Sally and Margie.

The curtains dropped instantly, blocking the women from view. But Kelly knew they were still there. Watching. Hoping to see something worth gossiping about.

"So? Is it a deal?" Micah asked.

Kelly sighed. This had been all her idea, after all. "Deal."

She moved to the side of the truck and Micah reached up to grab her at the waist. His hands were big and strong and hot enough to sear her skin right through the fabric of her shirt. He lifted her out of the truck bed as if she weighed nothing and then let her slide slowly along his body until she was standing on her own two feet again.

By the time her feet hit the ground, Kelly's insides were sizzling and her brain was fogging over. Her hands at his shoulders, she stared up into his brown eyes and read a wild mix of desire and amusement there. She couldn't have said why that particular combination appealed to her, but it did. "Well," she asked after a long minute of simply staring into each other's eyes, "are you going to kiss me?"

"Nope."

Surprised, she tried to pull away, but his hands only tightened on her waist. "Fine. But I thought you wanted a kiss for a favor."

"Yeah," he said, his gaze sliding over her face before meeting hers again, "but this time, *you* kiss *me.*"

Another swirl of hot nerves inside, but she had to admit it was only fair. He'd surprised her with their first kiss, and now she wanted to surprise him with just how hot a kiss could be if she knew it was coming. Giving him a faint smile, Kelly went up on her toes and slanted her mouth over his.

He held on to her but didn't take the lead. This show was all Kelly's. She parted his lips with her tongue, slid into his mouth and felt his breath catch in his throat. She explored his mouth, tasting, plundering. Spearing her fingers through his hair, she turned her head slightly to one side and groaned as he finally surrendered to the fire building between them. He clutched her tightly to him and tangled his tongue with hers until Kelly's mind splintered and floated out of her head to blow away in the cold breeze.

"Niiiiccceee…" Terry's voice was no more than a buzz that Kelly barely registered.

Kelly's heart banged against her ribs. She held on to Micah because if she didn't, she'd have keeled over from the rush of sensations pouring through her. His hands fisted at her back and held her so tightly to him she felt the hard length of him pressing into her belly. She rubbed against him, torturing them both. Knowing he felt what she felt, wanted what she wanted, only made her own feelings that much deeper. More intense.

God, she wanted to feel his skin beneath hers. She wanted to feel his heavy weight on top of her. Feel his hard body sliding into hers…

"Um, guys?" Terry's voice came again, hesitant

but insistent. Then she got louder, demanding they hear her. "*Guys!* You realize you're about to get way out of control right in the front yard?"

In a daze, feeling a little drunk, Kelly pulled her head back and turned to look blearily at her friend. "What?"

"Damn." Terry fanned herself with both hands. "I think that's enough of a show for now or you'll kill Sally and Margie."

"What?" Kelly asked again, and then realization slammed into her, and she turned to Micah and dropped her forehead on his chest. She could hardly believe what had just happened. If Terry hadn't spoken up, who knows what might have happened? "Oh, God."

"Yeah," Micah said tightly as he struggled to even out his ragged breathing. "I think Terry's right. I'll just get those boards for you now. Where do you want them?"

"Okay, that's good. Um, right in front of the porch," she whispered, and he let her go. Amazing how *alone* she felt without the strength of his arms wrapped around her middle.

Still a little shaky, she leaned against the truck and watched while Micah lifted a few of the huge plywood sheets and, balancing them on his shoulder, carried them to the front of the Victorian. His muscles stretched and shifted beneath his shirt. His black jeans hugged his behind and his long legs, and her mouth went dry just watching him.

"Honest to God," Terry murmured in her ear, "if you don't jump that man immediately, you're not the brave, intrepid Kelly I know."

"It's not that easy," Kelly said, gaze locked on him.

"Why the hell not?" Terry gave Kelly's shoulder a nudge. "You want him. He clearly wants you. I almost went up in flames just watching, and I can tell you that after seeing that kiss, when I get home, I'm video chatting Jimmy and hoping he's alone."

"That's different," Kelly grumbled. "You're married."

"And you're *engaged*," Terry reminded her. "For God's sake, take advantage of it."

But that hadn't been part of their deal, Kelly told herself. Was it fair to try to alter their agreement now? Then she remembered the grinding pressure of his mouth on hers and knew that he'd be okay with changing the rules. The question was, could she keep her emotions separate from the physical desire engulfing her? And could she live with herself if she *didn't* act on what she was feeling?

Micah walked back across the yard for the next load and Kelly's gaze fixed on him. Black jeans. Black boots. Black T-shirt. Dark brown hair ruffling in the cold breeze. Brown eyes that met hers for one long, blistering moment.

And she knew that, complicated or not, deal or not, she had to have him.

* * *

Micah ignored the noise from the front of the house for the next two hours. He heard the constant hammering, the arguing between Kelly and Terry and told himself it had nothing to do with him. What did he care about haunted houses? Besides, he had work to do. If thoughts of Kelly and that kiss ever left him the hell alone.

Scowling, he glared at the computer screen, rereading what he'd just written. His heroine was in deep trouble and getting in deeper every second. She was wandering the woods, looking for a lost child, and had no idea there was a killer right behind her.

Grimly he kept typing, in spite of the fact that his jeans were so tight he felt he was going to be permanently injured. He kept tasting Kelly on his lips and told himself that it didn't matter. It had been for show. To impress the neighbors and show them that Kelly's fiancé was crazy about her. The fact that it had impacted *him* so much wasn't the point.

Points. Kelly and her points. What was it now, three to one with her in the lead? Hell, if she'd brought it up at the time, he'd have awarded her five more points for that kiss today. He felt like her mouth was permanently imprinted on his. If he lived to be a hundred, he'd still be able to bring back the taste of her and the feel of her in his arms while the cold wind danced around them.

"This isn't getting any work done," he muttered,

and stood up from the desk. It wasn't until that moment that Micah realized how quiet it was. The hammering had stopped, and there was no more good-natured shouting from Kelly and Terry.

He walked to the window and looked out. At that angle, all he could see were the tops of plywood panels the two women were fixing together and standing in front of the porch. But it seemed that work on the haunted house was over for the day. Good. No noise meant not being reminded of Kelly. With no thoughts of Kelly, maybe he'd get some pages written.

"Where did she go?" he muttered an instant later, drumming his fingers on the window frame. "And why do you care?"

He didn't, of course. Curiosity didn't translate into *caring*.

Shaking his head, Micah walked to the desk and it felt like the computer screen was glaring at him, mocking him for stopping in the middle of a damn sentence. Well, he didn't have to be insulted by his own tools. He slammed the laptop shut and stalked out of the office. Work wasn't happening. Relaxing wasn't happening. So he'd try a beer, the game on TV and a chance to shut off his mind. Micah took the stairs, then turned and headed for the kitchen.

He never made it.

Kelly stepped through the swinging door from the kitchen into the dining room and stopped dead when she saw him. Everything in Micah tensed and eased at the same time.

Her hair tumbled wild and wavy around her face and down over her shoulders. Her eyes were bright and locked on him like laser beams. Micah's breath caught in his chest as a tight fist of need closed around his throat.

"Surprised to see me?" she whispered.

"Yeah." He nodded. "A little. But then you seem to be full of surprises."

"I'll take that as a compliment," she said, and moved a couple steps closer to him.

"You should." Micah walked toward her, too, one slow step at a time. "I never know from one minute to the next what you're going to do." He didn't admit how much he liked that about her. Didn't mention that he saw her *everywhere*. That images of her were dancing through his brain 24/7. Hell, he didn't even like admitting that to himself, let alone her.

Kelly's eyes flashed and his insides burned.

"Like being here now for instance," Micah said quietly. "What're you doing, Kelly?"

"I came to ask you a question."

He blew out a breath. "What is it?"

"Pretty simple, really," Kelly said, moving still closer.

He could have reached out and touched her, but Micah curled his hands into fists to keep from doing exactly that. After that kiss this afternoon, he was sure that if he held on to her now, he might not let her go again.

"There's a lot of…tension between us, Micah."

He snorted. "Yeah, you could say that."

She kept talking as if he hadn't spoken at all. "I mean, that kiss today? I thought the top of my head was going to blow off."

Micah reached up and rubbed the back of his neck. "I felt the same."

"Good," she said, nodding. "That's good."

"Kelly…" He was at the ragged edge of his near-legendary control. Her scent was reaching for him, and the look in her spring-green eyes was tempting him to just let go. "What're you getting at?"

"Well, we're both grown-ups, Micah," she said, tipping her head back to look at him.

"Yeah," he said tightly. "That might be part of the problem."

She laughed shortly. "True."

Her hair fell in a red-gold curtain behind her, and a light floral scent that clung to her skin seemed to surround him. "But, since we *are* adults, there's a simple way to take care of that tension." She took a breath and held it. When she spoke again, the words tumbled from her in a rush. "I think we should just go to bed together. Once we do that, we'll both be able to relax and—"

Control snapped at the suggestion he'd been hoping for. Micah grabbed her, speared his fingers through her hair and held her head still for his kiss. He poured everything he felt into it. The un-bearable frustration that had tortured him for two months. The wild, frantic need that disrupted his sleep every night. The desire that pulsed inside him like an extra heartbeat.

She groaned, fueling the fire enveloping him, and kissed him back with the same fierce hunger that was clawing at him. Her hands moved up and down his back, up into his hair, then clutched at his shoulders.

Micah's brain simply shattered. He didn't need it anyway. The only thing either of them needed now was their own willing bodies. When Micah tore his mouth free of hers and gasped for air, Kelly grinned at him. "I guess that's a yes?"

Surprise after surprise.

"No, it's a *hell yes*," he corrected, then picked her up and slung her over one shoulder in a fireman's carry.

"Hey!" Hands against his back, she pushed up and swung her hair back in an attempt to see him. "What're you doing?"

He glanced back at her and rubbed one hand over her behind until she shifted in his grasp.

"This is faster. No time to waste," he told her, and headed for the stairs again.

"Right." She rubbed her own palms over his back, then down to his butt. "Hurry."

He took the stairs two at a time, his long legs making short work of the distance separating them from the nearest bed. He covered the hallway in a few long steps, walked into his bedroom and tossed her onto the mattress.

"Whoop!" She laughed as she bounced, then her gaze met his and all amusement fled. "Oh, I'm so glad you didn't say *thanks, but no thanks.*"

"Not a chance of that," Micah assured her, and yanked his T-shirt off over his head.

Kelly smiled, licked her lips and toed off her shoes before immediately tugging at the button and zipper of her jeans. She squirmed out of them, making Micah's mouth water at his first peek at the tiny triangle of pink lace panties she had on under those jeans.

She kept her gaze locked on his as she worked on the buttons of her long-sleeved shirt and slowly let it slide down off her arms. The pink lace bra matched the panties and displayed more of her breasts than it hid.

He couldn't look away from her. Every breath came loud and harsh in the room. Micah felt like he was straining against a leash that had held him in place for two long months. Now that it was ready to snap, he didn't know what to do first. Where to touch. Where to kiss. Where to lick. He wanted it all. When she took off the bra and panties then tossed them over her head to the floor, the leash finally snapped.

She lay there, her pale skin luminous against the forest-green duvet. Her hair spilled out around her head like a red-gold halo of silk. Her breasts were fuller than he'd imagined, but delicate, too, her dark rose nipples rigid with the desire pumping through her.

His mind simply went blank. Like a starving man suddenly faced with a gourmet feast, Micah froze, helpless to look away from the woman laid out in front of him like a dream.

"Micah...you're wearing too many clothes," she murmured, licking her lips.

"Right. I am." He peeled out of his clothes, and in seconds he was naked and covering her body with his. Her hands slid up and down his back, across his shoulders to his chest and then up to cup his face. When Micah kissed her again, their bodies moved against each other as if they both were looking for that skin-to-skin contact. To revel in the heat. To drown in it. As if to assure each other that they were finally going to ease the raging desperation that had chased them both through torturous days and long, sleepless nights.

He swept one hand down the length of her as he shifted, dragging his mouth from hers to trail kisses along the line of her jaw, the slim column of her throat. She sighed, gasped and arched up into him. Her legs tangled with his, smooth to rough, adding new sensations to those already crashing down on them.

He slid his hand across her abdomen, down her belly to the center of her. To the heat he needed to claim, to bury himself in. She jerked helplessly. To drive her higher, faster, Micah took one hard nipple into his mouth.

Instantly, Kelly writhed in his arms as if trying to escape even while she held his head to her breast to keep him from stopping. "Micah… Micah, this is too much."

"No," he whispered, "not nearly enough." He covered her damp, hot core with his hand and slid first one, then two fingers inside her. She arched into him and his mind splintered at the feel of her generous, oh-so-eager body shaking and twisting in his arms.

His lips, teeth and tongue worked her nipple as his fingers continued to push her toward a release they both needed so badly.

"Stop, Micah," she whispered brokenly.

He lifted his head, questions in his eyes. "You want me to stop?"

Shaking her head, she choked out a short laugh. "Not on your life. I just want more than your hand on me." She was breathless, eyes a little wild, and she'd never looked more beautiful. "If you keep touching me like that, I'm going to climax and I don't want to. Not without you inside me."

Relief flooded him. He'd have had to back away if she'd changed her mind, and Micah knew without a doubt that stopping would have killed him. Knowing that she was simply trying to hold back an orgasm gave him the freedom to push her beyond the ability to fight it.

"One now," he said, stroking that one sensitive nub at her core with his thumb. "More later."

"Oh…my…goodness…" Her fingers dug into his shoulders. Her hips rocked frantically into his hand. She planted her feet and lifted herself higher, higher. He watched as Kelly's eyes glazed. "Micah—I… What are you doing to me? I've never…"

Micah had never been with anyone like her before. What she felt echoed inside him. The taste of her filled him, the scent of her swamped him, and the shattered, hungry look in her eyes fed the fires inside him like nothing he'd ever experienced before.

He hadn't been prepared for this, he thought, frantic himself as he watched her body bow and twist. He'd thought it would be a simple matter of bodies meeting, doing what came naturally. Feeling that sweet flash of release and moving the hell on. But no woman had ever affected him like this. No woman had slipped beneath his defenses, made him crave *her* release as much as his own. He didn't know what any of it meant, and now wasn't the time for trying to figure it out.

Micah felt the first shudder take her, body rippling with too much sensation all at once. She fought for breath, grasping at his shoulders, digging her head back into the mattress, struggling for air as she screamed his name like a prayer to an indifferent god.

His own breath caught in his chest. Mouth dry,

heart hammering, body as tight as a bowstring, Micah set her down on the bed and shifted, reaching for the drawer of the nightstand. He pulled it open, grabbed a condom and ripped the foil packet. He had to have her. Now.

"Micah, that was—" She shook her head, at a loss for words. The smile that curved her lips shone in her eyes, as well. "I've never…" She stretched like a happy cat and damn near purred. Then she opened her eyes at the sound of foil tearing.

"Wow. You went out and bought condoms just in case?"

He shook his head. "Nope, had them with me."

"You *travel* with condoms?" she asked, surprise in her voice.

He glanced at her. "Doesn't everyone?"

"Hoping to get lucky, were you?"

"Babe," he admitted as he sheathed himself, "I'm a *guy.* I'm always hoping to get lucky."

Her grin spread as she held out her arms to him. "Well, since I think we're both pretty lucky at the moment, I can't really complain, can I?"

He returned her grin, and as he shifted to part her thighs and kneel before her, he quipped, "So, having a condom handy means a point for me, huh?"

"Oh," she teased, "I don't know about that. I mean *points* are serious business and—"

He slid into her heat, and she went instantly quiet as she shifted a little to accommodate him. Then she groaned and tipped her head back into the mattress.

"Yes," she said. "If you can keep making me feel like—*oh!*—this, definitely a point for you."

"I love a challenge," he whispered. Still smiling, he covered her mouth with his and tangled their tongues in a dance that mimicked the movements of their bodies. She gave as much as she took, Micah thought, and realized that for the first time he was with a woman who was completely herself. There was no pretense with Kelly.

Whatever she felt, she let him know. Her soft cries and whimpered moans told him exactly what she liked. She was a little wild and he liked it. His mouth moved on hers as his hips rocked, slipping into a rhythm that had her kissing him hungrily, sliding her hands up and down his back, dragging her nails across his skin.

When he was strangling for air, he lifted his head to watch her expressive face as he claimed her completely. Her body held his in a tight, hot embrace, and he gritted his teeth to keep from giving in to the urge to let go. He wanted this to last. Wanted to make her crazy before he finally gave them both what they needed most.

Outside, twilight stained the sky a deep violet. Inside, the only light was in her eyes as she stared up at him, a look of wonder in her gaze. Their hands met, fingers linked, and he felt it when her climax slammed into her. Her body arched, her heels dug into his lower back. She screamed his name, and Micah watched the inner explosions ripple across her face and felt more satisfaction himself than he could ever remember. His heart raced, and his body continued to move in hers, and only when the last of the tremors coursed through her did he let himself go, finally giving up control and diving into the maelstrom, willingly letting it take him.

Seven

Kelly didn't know how much time had passed. And truthfully, she couldn't have cared less. Her whole body was humming as if her finger was somehow stuck in a light socket and electricity was pouring through her.

Finally, though, when she thought she could speak again, she said simply, "Wow."

"Agreed." Micah's voice was muffled because his face was buried in the curve of her shoulder.

She smiled to herself and stared blankly up at the ceiling. Good to know that he was as shattered as she felt. Micah's body pressed her into the bed and she knew she should ask him to move, but it was so lovely to feel the heavy press of a man's body on hers after so long on her own.

At that thought, Kelly felt a pang of sorrow that peaked and ebbed inside her in seconds. *Sean.* She closed her eyes briefly, as if thinking about him now was a breach of trust, somehow. Which was just stupid and she knew it. But, until today, Sean was the only man she'd ever been with. Hardly surprising that thoughts of her late husband would rise up.

Sean and Micah were so very different in so many ways. Micah's body was stronger, bigger— in every way, she thought with a tiny stab of guilt for the comparison. But it wasn't just their physical differences that set them apart.

With Micah there was laughter along with the sex. Kelly smiled, remembering the teasing about points and traveling condoms. With Sean, lovemaking had been a serious business. Instead of romance and fun, she'd always felt as if Sean had had a mental checklist. *Turn lights off, check. Kiss Kelly, check. Tongue, check. Touch breasts, check.* Their times in bed together had been almost clinical, more of a task to be accomplished.

God, she couldn't believe she was even having these disloyal thoughts. Kelly had never told anyone how unsatisfied she'd been in her marriage. Not even Terry. Though she had loved Sean, until now Kelly had believed that she simply wasn't capable of the kind of orgasms that Terry described— *blinding, mind-shattering, earthshaking.* Because in her husband's arms, Kelly had never felt more than a tiny blip of pleasure. Before today, sex had been just a sense of closeness.

She'd had absolutely no idea that there was a tsunami of sensations she'd never experienced.

Kelly opened her eyes and looked at the man she still held cradled to her. In the first few moments with Micah, Kelly had discovered more, *felt* more than she ever had with her husband. And maybe, Kelly thought for the first time, that was the reason she hadn't been interested in going on dates, finding another man. Because being with Sean hadn't been all that great.

She'd long blamed herself for the lack of spark between her and Sean, assuming that she just wasn't experienced enough to really make things heated between them. Now she had to admit that maybe the truth was that she and Sean had been friends too long to make the adjustment to lovers.

"I can hear you thinking," Micah murmured. "Keep it down."

Kelly grinned, grateful he'd interrupted her thoughts. Silently she let go of the past and returned to this amazing moment and the man she'd shared it all with. "Are you sleeping?"

"Yes," he muttered.

She laughed and the motion had his body, still locked inside her, creating brand-new ripples of expectation. Stunned, she couldn't believe she was ready to go again after what had been the most staggering orgasm of her life. Kelly slid her hands up and down his broad back and lifted her hips slightly to recreate that feeling. Instantly she was rewarded with another tiny current of electricity.

He hissed in a breath, lifted his head and looked down at her, one eyebrow arched high. "You keep moving like that and we're going to need a new condom."

Naturally she wriggled again, deliberately awakening a wave of fresh need. Reaching up, Kelly cupped his face in her palms and asked, "How many condoms do you have?"

He rocked his hips against her and she gasped.

One corner of his mouth lifted. "I'm thinking not nearly enough."

Was it bad that her heart did a slow roll and flip at the sight of his smile? Was it dangerous that she wanted nothing more than to stay here, like this, with Micah smiling down at her, forever? Her heart pounded painfully in her chest and her whole body trembled as he sat back onto his heels, drawing her with him, keeping their bodies locked together.

"Oh, boy." She said it on a sigh as she settled onto Micah's lap. Face-to-face, their mouths only a kiss apart, Kelly was lost in the rich brown of his eyes. His body went deep. She *felt* him growing, thickening inside her, and she swiveled her hips, grinding her core against him to feel even more.

He bent his head to take her nipples, one after the other, into his mouth. Kelly looked blindly around the familiar room, trying to distract herself so she wouldn't climax as quickly this time. She wanted to draw this moment out as long as she could. So she looked at the forest-green walls, the white crown molding, the now-cold white-tiled fireplace and the chairs drawn up before it.

She'd lived here most of her life and knew every corner of the old Victorian; yet, she'd never been more alive than she was at that moment. Never been so in tune with her surroundings, with her own body and with the man currently setting her on fire with a desire sharper, richer than she'd known ever before.

He suckled at her as if trying to draw everything she was within him. Kelly surrendered to the moment, concentrating not on where she was but what was happening. His big hands scooped up her spine and into her hair, fingers dragging along her scalp. Kelly watched him at her breasts while that delicious tugging sensation shot through her body.

Another first. She'd never made love like this— sitting atop a man so that every stroke of his body into hers was like a match struck. Kelly went up on her knees and slid down slowly, taking him as deep as she possibly could.

When Micah groaned and lifted his head, staring into her eyes, she felt stronger than she ever had. She moved on him again, picking up a rhythm that tormented both of them, and every time she rocked on him, she swore she could feel him touch her heart.

Her breath came in sharp, short puffs as she rode that crest of building pleasure again. How could she have not known all there was to *feel*? To *experience*?

Micah's jaw was tight as he fought for control. He looked into her eyes and dropped his hands to her hips to guide her into a faster rhythm. Bracing her hands on his broad shoulders, Kelly bit her bottom lip, tossed her hair back and stared deeply into Micah's steady gaze. She couldn't look away. Couldn't stop the growing wave of sensation inside her. Sliding her hands from his shoulders, she ran the flat of her palms across the sharply defined muscles of his chest. She ran her thumbnails across his nipples and watched him shudder and grind his teeth in response and she felt…powerful. Knowing what she was doing to this strong man made her feel sexy. Desired.

On his knees, he pushed into her and she twisted on his lap, grinding her pelvis against his, torturing them both, hurrying them along the path to a climax that would, she knew, completely shatter her. She wanted it. More than anything. She raced blindly toward it.

"Micah," she whispered, still scraping her nails across his nipples, still looking into his eyes. "Go faster. Go harder."

"You're killing me," he ground out, then flipped her over onto her back. Still locked inside her, he drove himself into her, again and again, harder, higher, faster until neither of them could breathe easily. He lifted her legs, draped them across his shoulders and continued his relentless claiming of her.

Kelly shouted and fisted her hands in the duvet beneath her. The world was rocking wildly. He was so deep inside her she thought he might always be there. And she wanted that, too.

Again and again, they moved in a frantic dance designed to end in a splintering of souls, until the world shrank down to the bed alone and nothing outside the two of them mattered. He took her hard and fast and deep and she went with him eagerly.

Kelly called his name over and over again until it became a chant. Lifting her hands, she held on to his upper arms as he braced himself over her and dug her nails into his skin.

"It's coming. Come with me," she said brokenly, voice tearing like wisps of fog in a heavy wind. The tension inside her heightened unbearably. She moved into it, trying to throw herself at the pleasure waiting for her. "Now, Micah. Please, *now*."

"Come then," he ground out, staring into her eyes. "Let me see your eyes when I take you."

Her release slammed into her like a freight train. She forced her eyes to stay open. She wanted him to see what he was doing to her. What only he had ever done. She quaked and shivered and finally screamed his name in desperation.

And, before the last of the tremors shuddered

through her, he called out her name and stiffened as his body joined hers. Kelly held him as he took from her as much as he had given. Then he collapsed, bonelessly atop her, and, shattered, Kelly cradled him in her arms.

It was dark when Kelly woke up. She was a little stiff. A little sore. And a lot desperate for air. Micah was sound asleep on top of her. Couldn't really blame him for being wiped out, but as good as he felt on top of her, Kelly really needed to breathe easier. Shaking her head, she said, "Micah! Micah, roll over."

"What?" Groggy, he lifted his head and opened his eyes. Understanding instantly, he rolled to one side, keeping an arm locked around her middle. "I fell asleep."

"We both did." Taking a deep breath, she curled into his side and just managed to swallow a sigh of satisfaction. "What time is it, anyway?"

"Who cares?" He threw one arm across his eyes.

"Good point."

"Hey," he said. "Another point for me."

"That wasn't a point. That was just a figure of speech. So it's still three to two, my favor."

He smiled. "So I *did* get a point for all of this."

Kelly sighed. By rights she should have given him ten, twenty, even thirty points for everything he'd made her feel. "Oh, boy, howdy."

"I can live with that."

She laughed. "Okay, so, are you hungry? I'm hungry."

He opened one eye. "You're kidding."

"I never kid about food." She went up on one elbow and looked down at him. Oh, my, he was great looking when he was dressed, but *naked*? The man was droolworthy. Kelly shook her head. If she kept going down that path, she would start something that wouldn't get her fed.

And if she didn't eat soon, she wouldn't have the strength for everything else she wanted to do with Micah. Now that was motivation. "Come on, you've got to be hungry, too."

"Not enough to move anytime soon."

"Really?" Kelly sat up and stretched, feeling looser and more limber than she had in years. "I'm not tired at all. In fact, I feel energized. We should have done this a long time ago."

He stared up at her and frowned.

"What?"

"Seriously?" He studied her as if she were on a slide under a microscope. "You feel great and you're hungry. That's all you have to say?"

Confused, Kelly laughed. "What were you expecting?"

Propping himself up on both elbows, Micah tipped his head to one side. "So you're not going to say that you've been doing some thinking and that we should talk?"

"About what?"

"About your feelings," he said. "And how sex changes things between us and we should figure out where our *relationship* goes from here."

She would have laughed again, but he looked so serious she just couldn't do it. Shaking her head, Kelly held up one hand. "Wait. Is that what most women do? Have sex with you and then ruin it with...*talk*?"

He frowned. "Well, generally, yeah."

She didn't know whether to be insulted that he'd expected her to be like every other woman he'd met in his life—or to feel bad that he had to protect himself against wily women looking to hook him into a relationship he didn't want. So she did neither.

Kelly smiled, bent down and planted a quick, hard kiss on his mouth. "Well, then, I'm happy to surprise you again. I came to you, remember? All of this was *my* idea—"

"Well," he said, "in my defense, I'd had the same idea—I just hadn't approached you with it yet."

"Even if you had, it wouldn't matter." She shrugged. "We're two adults, Micah. We can have sex—really *good* sex—without it meaning hearts and flowers, right?"

Confusion shone in his eyes. "Well, yeah, it's just—"

"What's wrong now?" Hadn't she eased his mind yet?

"Nothing," he said, a scowl tugging at his lips.

"It's just, I'm the one who usually gives that little speech. It's weird being on the receiving end."

"Another first." Kelly took a deep breath then blew it out. "Well, I'm done talking. But I could really go for a sandwich."

She scooted off the bed, picked up his discarded T-shirt and pulled it over her head. God, she felt good. "You want one?"

"Sure," he said slowly, thoughtfully. "I could eat."

"Great. I'll see you in the kitchen." Kelly left the room and didn't stop walking until she was downstairs. Then she paused and looked back up toward the room where she'd left him.

She'd told him she didn't want to talk and that was true. What she didn't tell him was that she was starting to feel a lot more for him than she'd planned on. Maybe it was the way he was so hesitant about letting people in. Maybe it was the half smile that curved his mouth so unexpectedly. She didn't know exactly what it was that was growing inside her, but Kelly was pretty sure that she was headed for trouble.

For the next few days, Micah and Kelly developed a routine that worked for both of them.

Micah spent the mornings working, building his novel page by page while Kelly raced from one job to the next. In the afternoons, they worked together on her Halloween project.

And every night they were together at the Victorian in Micah's bed.

Micah glanced over at Kelly now as she showed three kids how to roll black paint onto the plywood sheets. A reddish-gold ponytail hung down between her shoulder blades and swung like a metronome with her every movement. She wore her favorite worn jeans with the rip on the right thigh, black work boots and a faded red sweatshirt with the slogan Women Do It Better scrawled across the front. There was black paint on her cheek and a smile on her face as she listened to some long, involved story one of the kids told her.

A sharp stab of desire hit Micah so hard, so fast he nearly lost his breath. Hell, the skies were gray and there was an icy wind sliding through the nearby canyon, and Micah felt like his insides were blazing.

He and Kelly had thought to ease the sexual tension between them by sleeping together. Instead, they'd poured gasoline on a smoldering fire and started an inferno. Micah wanted Kelly all the time now. She was constantly on his mind. Her image, her scent, the harsh cries she made when he was inside her, pushing her over the edge.

This had never happened to him before. He should have known, he told himself, that Kelly would be unlike any woman he'd ever met. That had to be why he found her so intriguing. It was the newness factor. Her unpredictable nature. Her ability to keep him guessing, always on his toes. Hell, she *still* hadn't started that whole *we should talk* conversation he kept expecting. And a part of him was waiting for that shoe to drop.

There was no one else in his life who could have gotten him to stand out in the cold putting up plywood walls for a neighborhood Halloween maze. Shaking his head, he didn't know whether to be impressed by her or ashamed of himself.

He emptied his mind and took a good look at what they were building. It wasn't really a haunted house, but more of a passageway kids would have to go through to collect candy on Halloween night. Black walls, fake spiderwebs, a recording of scary sounds and voices, there were also going to be black lights to cast weird shadows and a few ghoulish mannequins to finish it all off.

If anyone had told him a year ago that he'd be in a small town in Utah building scary Halloween stuff, he would have called them crazy. Yet, here he stood.

"How the hell did this happen?" he muttered.

"You said a bad word," Jacob said, frowning up at him.

He looked down at the little boy and sighed. For some reason, this one particular kid had adopted Micah. Apparently, since Micah had taken the kid to visit his pumpkin, that had forged a bond. At least in Jacob's mind.

"What?"

"A bad word," the boy said. "You said *hell*."

"Oh." He rolled his eyes. Really had to watch that, he supposed. But then he wasn't exactly accustomed to dealing with children, was he? Even when he was at Sam and Jenny's place, Micah didn't spend much time with their two kids. In his defense, Isaac was a baby, so the kid didn't have much to say. And Annie, he realized suddenly, was Jacob's age.

Funny. He'd always told himself that he didn't pay attention to Sam's kids because he had no idea how to act with them. But he and Jacob got along so well that the boy had unofficially adopted him. That made him wonder if maybe he should have tried harder to get to know Sam's daughter, Annie.

But at the same time, Micah remembered that he didn't *like* kids. He didn't ask Jacob to hang around all the time, did he? Micah didn't want to get close to anyone. Had, in fact, spent most of his life avoiding any kind of connection.

And how has that worked out for you?

He glanced at the little boy kneeling beside him and gave an inner sigh. Now he had to remember to watch his language because a child had decided the two of them were best friends.

"Yeah, well," Micah said finally. "I shouldn't have said the bad word. And don't you say it."

Jacob's eyes went wide. "Oh, I won't cuz once Jonah said *damn* and Mommy made him go sit in his room and he *cried*."

And the ten-year-old probably wouldn't appreciate his little brother sharing that bit of news. Still, nodding sagely, Micah said, "Learn from your brother's mistakes then. Now," he added, "hold the hammer in both hands and hit the nail."

Micah yanked his fingers out of the way just in time, as Jacob's aim was pretty bad. But the grin on the kid's face was infectious. He was clearly proud of himself and loved being thought of as big enough to help like the other kids. Micah smiled at the kid and wondered again just how this had happened to him.

"Can I do another one?" Jacob asked, turning his face up to Micah's.

"Sure," he said, glancing at the bent, smashed nail. Micah would fix them later. For now, let the kid feel important. Memories of his own childhood swept through Micah's mind in an instant. Ignored by adults, he'd taken advantage of their disinterest and learned how to become invisible. He didn't cause trouble. Didn't stand out for good or bad reasons. And because he'd spent every minute trying to not be seen, not once had he *ever* felt important. To anyone.

Micah held out another nail and watched Jacob situate it just right. "Be careful. If you smash your fingers Kelly will get mad."

Jacob laughed delightedly. "No, she won't. But I can be careful."

When his cell phone rang, Micah grabbed it from

his back pocket and looked at the screen. "Can you be careful on your own?"

"I can do it. I'm not a baby."

"Right. I forgot." The phone rang again and Micah stood up. "I'll be right back," he told Jacob, then answered the phone as he stepped away from all the hammering and kids' high-pitched voices. "Hey, Sam."

"Hey, yourself," his agent countered. "You haven't called to whine in a few days so I figured you were dead."

Reluctantly Micah laughed. "That's not bad. Giving up the agent life to hit the stand-up circuit?"

"I could," Sam said. "Annie thinks I'm funny."

"Your daughter is three." Micah kept walking until he was ten feet from the small crowd gathered in front of the Victorian. The breeze was stronger out here, without the big house giving any shelter. "She thinks your evil cat is funny."

"Sheba's a perfectly nice cat," Sam pointed out. "With excellent judgment. She likes everyone but you."

"She knows I'm a dog person," Micah said, then frowned. Hell, he didn't know if he was a dog person. He'd never had a pet. Not that he cared. It was just odd to suddenly realize that. But he was always traveling. How was he supposed to take care of an animal if he didn't have a home?

"Great, I'll get you a puppy."

"Do it and die," Micah told him, though it surprised him to realize that a puppy didn't sound like such a bad idea. He scrubbed one hand over his face as if he could wipe away thoughts that had no business in his mind. "If you're calling about the book, it's still coming slowly."

Mostly because instead of just imagining what it might be like to have sex with Kelly, he was spending most of his free time remembering what they'd done together the night before. Hell, it was a wonder he got *any* work done.

"Yeah, this isn't about the book," Sam said. "I'm flying out to California in a couple days. I've got a Friday meeting with an indie publishing house."

Thanks to the internet, independent publishers were springing up all over the place. Most started and disappeared within a span of a few months— just long enough to fulfill and then crush would-be writers' dreams. But a few started small and built a strong list of writers and grew into houses with good reputations and steady sales.

Micah's gaze shifted to Kelly. She was bent over, helping Jacob's older brothers and a girl from down the street apply layers of black paint to plywood. The curve of her behind drew his gaze unerringly, and Micah had to look away for his own sanity.

He started paying attention again just in time.

"So," Sam was saying, "I thought you might want to fly out for the weekend. Take a break from small-town life and visit with an old friend."

It sounded like a great idea to Micah. He'd been

here in Banner for more than two months and he could do with a good dose of city life. Plush hotel, room service, noise, people…

"Sold," he said abruptly, then looked at Kelly again. She tossed her ponytail and laughed as Jacob's big brothers started painting each other. Looking at her wide smile, he could only think about getting her away from her home ground. Into some plush, luxurious life where he could seduce her nonstop. "But I won't be coming alone."

"Yeah?" He actually heard the intrigued smile in Sam's voice.

"Thought I'd bring my fiancée with me." He grinned, anticipating Sam's reaction. He wasn't disappointed.

A couple of long seconds filled with stunned silence ticked past before Sam sputtered, "Your *what*?"

"Can't get into it right now. I'll explain when I see you," Micah said, and had to admit he was enjoying leaving Sam hanging on the information front. "Where do you want to meet?"

"I'm staying at the Monarch Beach Resort in Dana Point, and who is this fiancée and when did this happen?"

"Got it," Micah said, ignoring the questions. "When's your meeting?"

"I'm flying in early Friday for a meeting that afternoon. But I'll be staying until Sunday."

"Okay." Micah did some fast figuring. It was

Tuesday now—he had plenty of time to arrange for a suite at the hotel and a private jet to get him and Kelly to Orange County. All he had to do was convince her to leave town for a few days. He had confidence in his ability there. "I'll see you then."

"You are *not* going to leave me hanging with no information," Sam complained. "Do you know what'll happen if I go home with this news and no details? Jenny will hound me."

Micah laughed. "Sounds perfect."

"You're gonna pay for this—"

Micah hung up and enjoyed it. Sure, Sam would find a way to get revenge, he told himself. But that's what good friends were for, right?

His gaze locked on Kelly. She must have felt him staring, and something inside him turned when she met his gaze and smiled at him. Her eyes were shining, the curve of her delicious mouth was tempting and when she turned back to the kids and bent down, his gaze locked on her behind again. The woman really had a world-class butt.

His body went tight and hard in an instant. Yeah. A few days away from here. No work interfering for either of them. Just relaxing and enjoying each other. What could be better?

Going online, Micah went to the hotel's website and reserved the Presidential Ocean Suite. He stayed there whenever he was in Southern California and he knew that Kelly would love it. The hotel was top-of-the-line, and this room in particular was damn impressive, with a private balcony that offered sweeping views of the Pacific. Micah smiled to himself as he imagined her on that terrace, the wind in her hair, moonlight making her bare breasts seem to glow. Naked with only the sky, the stars and the sea as witnesses. That's how he wanted her.

All he had to do now was find a way to convince her to take a break from her many responsibilities.

Kelly was flabbergasted.

One of her grandmother's favorite words, it was the *only* one that fit this situation, Kelly told herself. In fact, she was so stunned she couldn't think of a thing to say. And that was so unusual for her, she couldn't remember the last time it had happened.

Micah's invitation had come out of the blue and she'd instantly agreed. True, she had to rearrange the jobs she had lined up, but the chance to get away with Micah was one she didn't want to miss. Being with him was so important to her she was already worrying about what it would be like when he eventually left. But, until then, she wanted to be with him every minute she could be.

She and Terry had made an emergency shopping run to Salt Lake City. It had taken them hours, since Terry had insisted on hitting every single boutique and dress shop in the city, but it had been worth the trip. In her suitcase now, Kelly had clothes suited to a five-star resort.

As soon as Micah told her about the Monarch

Bay Resort, Kelly had looked it up online so she'd have some idea of where she'd be staying. The hotel was lovely, elegant. And completely intimidating.

First there had been the limo ride to the airport, then they had been ushered to a private concourse and escorted onto the jet Micah had chartered. Kelly had felt like a queen, lounging in the supple blue leather chairs set into conversation areas. *So* much better than flying like a sardine in an overcrowded can.

She and Micah had sipped champagne and nibbled on strawberries during the short flight. The limo ride to the hotel hadn't flustered her and she'd idly wondered if she was already getting accustomed to being spoiled. But walking into this hotel, where the staff called Micah by name and rushed to do his bidding, and then this spectacular suite… Kelly was simply overwhelmed.

The Presidential Ocean Suite was breathtaking. There was a fireplace, several overstuffed couches and chairs in soft pastels. The carpet was thick and the color of sand. There were vases filled with fresh yellow roses, and there were French doors leading to the private terrace.

The bedroom was huge, with its own fireplace and another set of French doors leading to the balcony they shared with no one. There were crystal chandeliers over the dining table and the bathroom was bigger than her whole cottage back home, with a tub wide and deep enough to swim in and a shower built for a cozy party of five or six, with built-in benches that made Kelly think of any number of things she and Micah could do on them.

And *when* had she become so interested in sex?

Answer, of course—the first time Micah kissed her. He'd created a monster. Smiling to herself, Kelly said simply, "Micah, this is just…amazing. The whole day has been—" She broke off, at a loss for words for the first time in forever. "I wouldn't have missed this for anything."

She walked toward the open terrace doors and caught the shimmer of sunlight on the deep blue of the ocean as it stretched out into eternity. A soft sea breeze danced into the room, ruffling the sheer white curtains.

"I'm glad you came," he said.

"So am I."

Kelly turned to him. He wore black slacks, a dark red dress shirt with the collar open and a black sports coat. He looked comfortable in his surroundings and she realized that *this* was how he lived all the time. He'd told her that he moved from hotel to hotel when he was working, but somehow, even knowing he was rich and famous, she hadn't considered that the hotels he was talking about were really more like palaces.

Kelly tried to imagine living in a place like this and just couldn't do it. The thought of trying to fit into this kind of lifestyle on a daily basis was exhausting. For Kelly, this was an aberration. A step outside her own reality. Okay, more than a step. A *leap*. But the reality was this: as gorgeous as this place was, as glad as she was that she'd come away with Micah, Kelly felt like an interloper here. But, for the next few days, she was going to pretend that she *did* belong, because there was nowhere else she'd rather be.

His gaze locked on her. "Did I tell you before we left that you look beautiful today?"

Kelly flushed, relishing the heat that always raced through her when Micah was near. And now she was doubly glad she and Terry had done so much shopping. Her new black slacks, white silk blouse and deep green brocade vest looked good on her, she knew. And she didn't want to *look* as out of place here as she felt. "You did tell me. Thank you."

He walked across the room to her, took her hand and then led her to the French doors. Stepping onto the terrace, she took a quick look around at the earth-toned tile floor, the table and chairs in one corner and the pair of lounge chairs complete with deep blue cushions and red pillows.

"It just keeps getting better and better," she murmured, and, letting go of his hand, walked to the iron railing and looked out at the sea. The ocean was a deep blue with gold glints of sunlight shining on its surface. Boats with jewel-toned sails skimmed along the waves while surfers closer to shore rode their boards with a grace she envied.

A soft breeze tossed her hair across her eyes. She plucked it free and sighed. "It's like a fairy tale."

"I've pictured you here," he said, and when she turned to look at him, she found his gaze locked on her. "Standing just there, the wind in your hair, a smile on that incredible mouth."

Her heartbeat skittered. "And is the reality as good?"

"Almost," he said, moving in close.

"Only almost?" Her eyebrows lifted and she laughed softly.

"Well, when I pictured you standing there, I was seeing you naked in the moonlight," he admitted, pulling her up against him.

A curl of damp heat settled at her core, and Kelly lifted her head to meet his gaze. Hunger shone in his eyes as he slid his hands down to cup her bottom and hold her tight to his erection. What was it about this man that turned her into a puddle of desires she'd never known before? Why was it he could touch her and send her up in flames? How could one smile from him turn her heart upside down?

She was very much afraid she knew the answers to all of those questions. But now wasn't the time to explore it. The next few days were just for them. To be together. To revel in each other. She didn't want to waste a minute of it.

"Well," she said, when she could breathe past the knot in her throat, "it's important to make dreams come true. So tonight…"

He hissed in a breath through gritted teeth and held her even tighter to him. "That's a date," he promised, then deliberately took a step back, groaning. "But if I want to show you anything of California, we'd better get going. How about we go down, pick up the car I've got waiting and drive up the coast?"

At that moment, she would have gone with him anywhere.

Eight

Micah took her up the coast to Laguna where they parked the car and walked along Pacific Coast Highway. They popped into art galleries, bought ice cream from a vendor and swayed in time to a street performer's smooth, slow saxophone performance.

Early October in California meant it was still warm, and with the sun shining down on them, the day couldn't have been more perfect. Then he spotted something in a shop window.

"Come with me," he said, taking Kelly's hand and pulling her into the cool quiet of the jewelry shop. The interior of the shop was cool and dimly lit so that the jewels in the glass display cases could shine like stars in the night beneath lights fixed to the underside of the cabinets. There was a dark red rug on the wood-plank floor, and a grandfather clock ticked loudly into the hushed quiet.

"Micah, what're you doing?"

"I saw something I want to get." He signaled an older man behind the gleaming glass cases filled with diamonds and gemstones.

"May I help you?" He wore round, wire-rimmed glasses. His gray hair was expertly trimmed, and his pin-striped suit complete with vest made him look as though he'd stepped out of the nineteen forties.

"Yeah." Micah glanced at Kelly as she wandered down the glass cases, admiring everything within. Turning back to the man in front of him, he said, "The emerald necklace in the window."

The man brightened. His eyes sparkled and a tiny smile curved his mouth. "One of our finest pieces, sir. One moment."

Kelly wandered back to Micah and leaned into him. "What're you buying?"

"A gift for someone," he said, leaving it at that as the man came back, laid the emerald necklace out on a black velvet tray and waited for their admiration.

"Oh, my, that's gorgeous," Kelly whispered, as if she were in church.

"It is, isn't it?" Micah liked the look of it himself, but he was more glad that Kelly approved of it, too. Square cut, the emerald was as big as his first thumb joint. The setting was simple, with platinum wire at the gemstone's corners and twin diamonds on either side of it, the stone hung on a delicate platinum chain. And the emerald itself, he thought, was exactly the color of Kelly's eyes. That's what had caught his attention in the first place. "Okay, I'll take it."

The older man's eyebrows lifted but, otherwise, he remained cool and polite. "Of course. Would you like it gift wrapped?

"Not necessary," Micah said, reaching for his wallet and then his credit card. He didn't bother to ask the price. It didn't matter, anyway.

"I'll take care of it straight away," the man said, then looked at Kelly. "I hope you enjoy it." Then he scurried away to ring up the sale, clearly wanting the business done before Kelly talked Micah out of the purchase.

"Oh," she said to the man's back as he left, "it's not for me…"

Her voice trailed off as Micah lifted the necklace from the black velvet and turned to her.

Eyes wide, Kelly looked horrified as she took a step back. "Micah, no."

Again, she surprised him. She hadn't even considered the possibility that the necklace was for her. "You said you liked it."

"Well," she said, "I'd have to be blind *and* stupid to not like it. That's not the point."

"You're right," he said, pushing past her reservations. "The point is, I want you to have it." He stepped behind her, laid the jewel at the base of her neck and ordered, "Lift your hair."

She did, but all the while she was shaking her head. "You can't just buy me something like this out of the blue—"

"Well," he said, voice low and teasing, "you did tell your grandmother that we were going to New York for a ring, so…"

"Micah." She turned her head to look at him, and he smiled at her to ease the worried look in her eyes.

When the necklace was secured around her neck, he moved to stand in front of her. The emerald shone like green fire on her skin and he felt a swift tug of satisfaction seeing her wearing it. "It looks perfect."

"It would look perfect on a three-legged troll," Kelly argued, but her fingers reached up to touch the stone and her gaze slipped to a mirror on the counter to admire it. "It's beautiful, Micah. Seriously. But you don't have to do this. Buy me things, I mean."

No, she wouldn't expect that from him and he found that…refreshing. Most of the women he'd ever been with had anticipated trinkets like this. They'd oohed and aahed over jewelry-store windows or even, on occasion, dragged him inside to let him know in no uncertain terms which piece they'd most like to have. But Kelly didn't want anything from him. Didn't demand anything. She was happy just being with him, and that had never happened before.

And maybe that was why Micah had felt compelled to buy her that damn necklace. He wanted her to have something to remember him by. In a few months, he'd be gone from her life, but every time she looked at that necklace, she'd remember today and she'd…what? *Miss him?* Had anyone, anywhere ever missed him? Had he ever wanted them to? Questions for another time, another place, he told himself.

"I wanted you to have it," he said simply. "It's the same color as your eyes."

"Oh, Micah…" Those big beautiful green eyes filled with tears and, just for a second, he panicked. But Kelly blinked the moisture back and lifted her chin. "You don't want to make me cry. I look hideous when I cry. I'm a sobber. I don't do delicate weeping."

Of course she wouldn't cry. He chuckled—how could he not? Kelly was one in a million at everything. "Good to know. I'll make a note. No making Kelly cry."

A wry smile curved her mouth briefly, then her shoulders slumped and a defeated sigh escaped her. "I can't stop you from doing this, can I?" she asked, still touching the cold, green stone.

"Already done, so no."

Nodding, she took a breath, let it out again and said, "Fine. Am I allowed to thank you?"

"Only briefly," he told her warily.

"Thank you, Micah," she said, going up on her toes to lay a soft, slow kiss on his mouth. "I've never owned anything more lovely. Whenever I wear it, I'll think of you."

His heart jolted. It was just what he'd wanted, yet hearing her say it he could almost hear the "goodbye" in her voice. He hadn't thought it would bother him, but it did. For the first time in his adult life, he wasn't looking forward to moving on. Frowning, he told himself he would. He had to. Eventually. But Micah didn't want to think about endings today.

Looking at her, the pleasure in her eyes, an emerald at her throat and a smile on that fabulous mouth of hers, all he could say was, "I'll think of you, too."

And he knew he'd never meant anything more.

Later that night, Kelly did a quick spin in place on her three-inch heels, sending the skirt of her new black dress flying. Then she stopped and looked up at Micah. "Today was so lovely. Thank you, Micah."

He shrugged. "It was fun."

It was a revelation, she thought but didn't say. She'd seen Micah in a whole new light. He was famous. Rich. Important. Everywhere they went, people scrambled to please him. Fans—mostly women—had stopped him on the street to coo over him, completely ignoring Kelly's presence. And she'd seen his reaction to all of the notoriety. It all made him uncomfortable. Sure, he was polite to everyone, but there was a cool detachment in everything he did that told Kelly he'd much prefer going unnoticed.

Micah lived a life that was so far removed from Kelly's they might as well have been on different planets. But, for now anyway, they were together. And maybe that was all she should think about.

She strolled across the terrace to the railing and lifted her face into the sea breeze that was soft and cool. Turning her head to him, she said, "I thought the maître d' at dinner was going to cry when you signed his book for him."

Micah poured them each a glass of champagne and carried them to her. Handing her one, he had a sip of his own. "I couldn't believe he had it with him at work."

She laughed and took a drink of the really fabulous wine. Shaking her hair back from her face, she sighed. "I can't believe I'm here. Not just California," she amended. "But here… Here. In this beautiful hotel. With you."

"I'm glad you are," he admitted, then frowned slightly as if he'd like to call the words back.

But it was too late, because Kelly heard them and held them close in her heart. He might not want to care about her, but he did. For now, that was enough for her. Neither of them had gone into this expecting anything but a release of sexual tension. And if she was feeling…more, then she'd just keep that piece of info to herself. He wouldn't want to hear it and she wasn't ready to admit it, anyway.

Pushing those thoughts out of her mind, Kelly turned from the railing, walked to the table and set her champagne flute down. When she turned back to Micah, she smiled and reached behind her back for the zipper. "I think we made a date for this terrace tonight, didn't we?"

She saw his grip on the fragile stem of the flute tighten. "Yeah. We did, didn't we?"

The zipper slid down with a whisper and she lifted both hands to hold the deeply scooped bodice of the dress against her. "And you're sure no one can see us?"

He took a drink and speared her with a look that was so hot, so barely contained, his brown eyes burned with it. "Private terrace. No neighbors. Empty ocean."

"Okay then." Kelly took a breath and let the dress drop to pool at her feet. She'd never done anything like this, and she felt both excited and exposed. But Micah's gaze on her heated her through, and she forgot about feeling self-conscious and instead enjoyed what she was doing to him.

On that shopping trip with Terry, Kelly had indulged in some new lingerie, as well. His expression was all she'd hoped for.

Micah's gaze moved up and down her body before settling on her eyes again. "You're killing me."

"You like?" He more than liked and she knew it.

"Yeah," he ground out. "You could say so. One point for the black lace."

Kelly grinned. "Nice! That makes it four to two, my favor."

"You keep dressing like that, I'll give you all the points you want."

She shook her head slowly and said, "But didn't you say that in your dream I was naked?"

"So you *are* trying to kill me."

"No," she assured him. "Just torture you a little." Slowly she peeled out of the black lace bra, dropping it onto the nearest chair. And, leaving her high heels on, she slipped out of the matching scrap of her panties and stood there with the ocean breeze drifting across her skin like a lover's hands.

"Well," she asked softly, "as good as the dream?"

"Better," he told her, and bent to take a kiss while his hands cupped her breasts, rolling her nipples between his thumbs and forefingers.

Kelly groaned and leaned into him, loving the feel of his hands on her skin. The taste of his mouth on hers. She felt completely wicked and absolutely wonderful.

He dropped one hand to her core and she parted her thighs for his touch. Micah had shown her more about herself, what her body was capable of, than she'd ever have believed possible. And now she wanted him all the time. Craved what happened between them when they were together. He stroked her, explored her, and she whimpered with need as an oh-so-familiar tension crept through her.

His thumb moved over that one sensitive spot and she gasped, moving her hips, trying to feel more, faster. He pushed one finger, then two, inside her and Kelly groaned again, clutching his shoulders, holding on while her body went on another wild ride courtesy of Micah Hunter.

The cold air brushed against her while his warm hands stoked fires inside her. Over and over, he touched, caressed, until she was just on the brink of a shattering climax. Then he stopped and she nearly shrieked.

"Micah—don't—"

"Wait." He lifted her, plopped her onto the table then, as she watched, he parted her thighs and knelt in front of her.

"What're you— Oh, Micah…"

Beneath her, the heavy metal table was cold against her behind, but she didn't feel cold. She felt as if she were on fire. Then Micah covered her center with his mouth and Kelly cried out in surprised pleasure. His lips, tongue and teeth drove her crazy. She threaded her fingers through his hair and held him to her as he continued his delicious torment.

He licked and suckled at the very heart of her, and the sensations rising inside her were powerful. Overwhelming. She had to hold on to him or she was sure she would have simply fallen off the face of the earth. She rocked helplessly in place as he pushed her so high there was no higher to go. Then the crash came and Kelly cried his name in a broken voice and let the sound drift away into the night wind.

Still trembling, she locked her eyes on his as he stood up and looked down at her. "Point to you," she whispered. "That was—"

"Four to three then," he said, scooping her off the table to cradle her close. "I'm catching up."

She smiled because she felt so darn good, but Kelly looked up at him through glazed eyes as she admitted in a whisper, "I've never— I mean no one…"

"I know what you meant," he said softly, his gaze locked with hers. "And if you're interested, there are a lot more firsts headed your way."

"I love to learn," she said, reaching up to briefly cup his face in the palm of her hand. Kelly laid her head on his chest as he carried her through the spacious living area into their bedroom.

Whatever he had in mind, Kelly was ready for it.

The following night, Micah and Kelly had dinner with Sam and Jenny Hellman, then the four of them took a walk around the hotel property. Both women were strolling slowly ahead of the men, and Micah could only guess they were still bonding over their favorite romance author.

Since Sam and Jenny had arrived, the four of them had spent a lot of time together, and Micah was pleased at how well Jenny and Kelly were getting along. Though why it mattered, he told himself, he couldn't have said. It wasn't as if they were all going on vacation together. And unless Sam and Jenny rented the Victorian for ski season again, they wouldn't be seeing each other after this weekend. Once Micah had moved on, none of the others would have any reason to meet. So why did it matter to him that the people he was closest to were becoming friends?

Hell, he didn't know. But that was typical. Since meeting Kelly, Micah had felt off his game. Off balance. And she was doing it to him. Micah's gaze locked on Kelly. She wore a bright yellow dress that made her look like a lost sunbeam in the night. Her hair was long and loose and the wind kept lifting it, as if teasing her. Something inside him stirred and warmth spread through his chest.

"You're sleeping with her, aren't you?"

"None of your business," Micah said tightly, and he knew that was as good as saying *yes*.

"Ah, touchy." Sam nodded thoughtfully. "That's interesting."

"What're you talking about?" Micah kept his gaze straight ahead because looking at Kelly was more fun than looking at Sam.

"Just that you've never minded talking about your women before…"

Micah ground his teeth together. "She's not one of my women," he said. "She's Kelly."

"Also interesting." Sam smiled to himself. "Getting attached, huh?"

"No." He was definitely not getting attached. Of course he cared about her. But there was nothing more than that because he wouldn't allow it. "Leave it alone, Sam."

"Not gonna happen." His old friend punched him in the shoulder and said, "For the first time, you've brought a girl home."

Micah snorted. "Are you crazy?"

"Come on. We both know Jenny and I are as close to family as you've got, and here we are, the four of us, bonding nicely. So I think that says something."

"And I think you should stick to being an agent," Micah told him. "Because the fiction you dream up sucks."

Sam laughed and waved one hand at his wife when Jenny turned around to look at them. "Why not just admit that you and Kelly have something good together?"

Micah sighed and fixed his gaze on Kelly again. The way her hair fell around her shoulders. Her long legs, the way that yellow dress clung to her curvy body. Everything about her appealed to him. And that was enough to make him wary. She was the only woman he'd ever met who had tempted him to look deeper. That made her dangerous.

"Because what we have is temporary." Saying

it aloud reinforced what he knew was pure truth. There was no future here.

"Well, I like her."

"Yeah," Micah said grimly. "So do I."

"Well, you don't sound too happy about it."

Micah scowled and wasn't sure if he was directing the expression at his friend or himself. "Why should I be? You know as well as I do I'll be leaving in a few more months."

Although, as he said it, Micah realized that moving on didn't sound as good as it usually did. Strange. Normally, after three months in one place, Micah was already getting restless. Making plans for where he would go next. Polishing up one book and already plotting the next. That was his life. Had been for years. And it worked for him, so why would he even consider changing it?

"And your point is…?"

"Don't say *point*."

"What?"

"Never mind." Micah shook his head. He'd never be able to hear that word again without thinking of Kelly. What were they now? Four to three. He remembered how he'd been awarded that last point and his body went hard as stone.

"This is *temporary*," he said again, emphasizing that last word, more for his own sake than for Sam's.

Sam stared at him as if he had three heads. "It doesn't have to be, that's what I'm saying. Hell, Micah, you're already engaged to her."

And this engagement would end just like the last one, he told himself. Sighing, Micah stuffed his hands into his slacks pockets. "We explained the whole thing to you. It's just a lie for Kelly's grandmother's sake."

"Lies can become truths."

Micah snorted. "No, they can't."

Sam shrugged. "Hey, look at it from my perspective. You guys get married, and Jenny, me and the kids have a place to stay every ski season."

"That's very thoughtful," Micah said wryly.

Sam smiled as he watched his wife stumble, catch herself and keep walking. "Jenny could trip over air, I swear." Sighing in exasperation, he said, "You and Kelly are good together, Micah. Why be in such a damn hurry to throw it away?"

Because he didn't know what to do with it.

"You don't buy gigantic emeralds for a woman you don't give a damn about—and thanks for that, by the way. Jenny's already reminded me that her favorite stone is a sapphire."

Micah laughed a little and it felt good to ease the tightness in his chest. "That's your problem. As for the emerald, I just wanted Kelly to have it. That's all."

They were walking through the hotel gardens and past the pool where a couple dozen people splashed in the aquamarine water. The sky was clear, the air was warm and the ocean breeze was cool and damp.

"Why?" Sam asked. "Why'd you want her to have it?"

"Because," Micah said in exasperation. "Just… because."

Sam laughed and Jenny turned around to look at him. He waved her off again and said, "Damn, Micah. No wonder I can get you so much money for your books. You've got a real way with words."

"Drop it, Sam."

Sam stopped. He was a couple inches shorter than Micah, a little heavier and a lot more patient. "Just admit it, man, she's got you. You care about her."

"Of course I care. What am I—a monster?" Micah stared out at the black ocean. "She's a nice woman." *Lame*, he thought. "We have a good time together." *They had a hell of a lot together.* "I like her." *Like. Care.* Hell, even he didn't believe him.

"Must be love."

Micah's head snapped around and his gaze burned into Sam's. "Nobody said anything about love."

Shaking his head, Sam mused, "Damn, you react to that word like a vampire does to a cross."

"I've got my reasons," Micah reminded him.

"Yeah, you do," Sam agreed. He leaned back against the railing behind him, folded his arms over his chest and said, "I'm the first to agree you had a crap time of it as a kid. So I get why you've closed yourself off up until now."

"I hear a 'but' coming," Micah mused.

Sam slapped his shoulder. "That's because you're a very smart man. So here it is. *But*, how long are you going to use that excuse?"

Micah shot him a look that would have had most people backing up with their hands in the air. Not Sam, though.

He gave Micah a bored smile. "Please. Don't bother giving me the Death Stare. It's never worked on me."

Micah rolled his eyes. True. "Fine. But my past is not an excuse, Sam. It's a damn *reason*."

"Because you had a miserable childhood you can't love anyone? That's just stupid." Shaking his head, Sam said, "It's like saying you never had a burger when you were a kid so now you can't have a Big Mac."

Micah scowled.

"Basically, buddy," Sam continued, "you're letting a crappy past mess with your present and future."

Micah ground his teeth together so hard it was a wonder they didn't turn into a mouthful of powder. Having his past reduced to a stupid analogy didn't help the situation any, and Micah felt compelled to defend his decisions on how he chose to run his life. If he wanted to be a footloose wanderer with no connections to anyone, that was his call, wasn't it? If it sounded lonely all of a sudden, that shouldn't be anyone's business but Micah's. And it had *never* mattered to him before, so he'd get over it. He liked being alone. Liked the freedom. Liked being able to pick up and move and have no one miss him. Right?

He frowned to himself over that last thought. Would Kelly miss him when he left? Would she think about him? Because he damn sure knew he would be thinking about her. *Just another reason to leave.*

"Wow," he said finally, "thanks for the analysis. How much do I owe you?"

"This one's on the house," Sam said, ignoring the sarcasm. "At some point," he paused. "Sorry. Used the word 'point' again, and someday you'll have to explain why we're not using it anymore."

Micah choked out a harsh laugh, but Sam wasn't finished.

"You have to decide if you want a life—or if you'd just rather be somebody else's victim for-freaking-ever."

"I'm not a damn victim," Micah muttered, in-sulted at the idea.

"Glad to hear it," Sam countered. "Now, what do you say we catch up with our women and go get a drink?"

"God, yes."

Sam hustled on ahead to catch up with Jenny and Kelly. Micah smiled in spite of everything as his friend offered each of them an arm and then led them off toward the hotel bar. Kelly turned her head to smile at him, and even at a distance Micah's heart gave a hard jolt.

He hadn't planned on any of this. All he'd wanted was a quiet place to work for six months. He hadn't asked to have Kelly come into his life. And now that she was there, he didn't know what to do about it. Sam meant well, but he couldn't understand what drove Micah. How the hell could he?

When you lived a life in the moment, tomorrows just never came into play. So, like always, Micah wouldn't look to the future—he'd just make the best of today.

Luxury hotels, limos and five-star restaurants made for a wonderful holiday, but after two weeks back at home, it all seemed like a pretty dream to Kelly.

As soon as they'd got home, she had stepped right back into her routine as if she'd never left, and that's how Kelly liked it. Her time away with Micah had been wonderful, but being here in her small town with him was perfect. She never took off the emerald necklace he'd given her so that, even when she was busy with her different jobs and Micah was shut away in the Victorian working on his book, it was like she had him with her everywhere she went.

Micah.

"You're doing it again."

Kelly jumped guiltily and grinned at Terry. "Sorry, sorry."

"Where were you?" Terry held up a hand. "Nope. Never mind. I know that look. I have it on my face constantly when Jimmy's home."

Kelly sighed a little, took a sip of her latte and

scooted closer to where Terry was rolling out dough for the next batch of cookies for her shop. The kitchen smelled like heaven and, like Terry, was organized down to the last cookie sheet stacked carefully on its rack.

Kelly kept her voice down so the girls running the counter out front couldn't hear her. "Terry, I've never— I mean, I had no idea that— Why didn't you tell me how amazing sex is?"

Terry laughed and shook her head. She picked out a cookie cutter and quickly, efficiently, stamped out a dozen shapes in the dough. Then she carefully lifted each of them to put on a cookie sheet for baking. "Honey, you were married, I thought you knew."

Feeling disloyal again, Kelly said, "It was never like this with Sean. I didn't know feelings could be so *big*. I mean," she said, sighed heavily and closed her eyes briefly to bring back the magic of Micah's hands on her skin. "What he does to me, it's…" She couldn't even find the words to explain and maybe that was best. "I just never want him to stop touching me."

Terry took a moment to fan herself with her hands. "Good thing Jimmy's calling me tonight because I'm dying of jealousy here." Then she took another long look at Kelly and said, "You're feeling guilty, too, aren't you? About Sean, I mean."

"A little." A lot. She didn't mean to compare the two men, but it was inevitable when what she felt with Micah was so much more than anything she'd ever known.

"You don't have to." Terry patted her hand. "Sean was a sweetie, but it's not like you two were legendary lovers or anything."

"I loved him," Kelly said softly.

"Of course you did," Terry agreed. "In a nice, comfortable, safe kind of way."

Was that what her marriage had been, Kelly wondered? Had she simply married Sean because he'd made her feel safe and settled? If Sean had lived, would they have stayed together? Would they have been happy? Kelly sighed again. There were no answers, and even if there were, they wouldn't change anything.

"He loved you, too," Terry said. "Enough, I think, to want you to be happy, Kelly. So, if Micah makes you happy, then yay him!"

Kelly picked up a finished cookie and took a bite, thinking about what Terry said. "He really does, you know? Every day, it just gets better between us. He's funny and crabby and kind and, God, the man has magic hands. In California, we were together all the time and…look." Leaning in, Kelly reached beneath the collar of her T-shirt and pulled out the emerald.

"Holy Mother of Cinnamon!" Terry all but leaped over the marble counter to lift the emerald with the tips of her fingers. She looked from the stone to Kelly and back again. "Is it real? Of course it's real. Rich guys don't buy junk. I didn't know emeralds *got* that big, for heaven's sake. And those are diamonds…

"Oh my God, I can't believe it took you two weeks to show me!"

Kelly laughed at her friend's reaction. "I just— it's kind of embarrassing. I mean, I told him not to buy it—"

"Of course you did." Terry sighed. "Why are you embarrassed to show me?"

"Because it sort of felt like bragging, I guess."

"Why wouldn't you want to brag about it?" Terry lifted the emerald and turned it back and forth so that the light caught and flashed off it. "That is amazing. If it was mine, I'd wear it stapled to my forehead so everyone would see it."

Laughing, Kelly realized she should have shown it to Terry as soon as she got home. But hiding the necklace wasn't just about not wanting to show off.

It was about the unshakable feeling she had that the emerald had been Micah's way of saying goodbye. Of letting her know that he would be leaving but he wanted her to have something to remember him by. Being Micah, it just had to be an emerald-and-diamond necklace, but the point was, she worried that he was already pulling away.

She'd noticed it more after Sam and Jenny had shown up. It was as if having his friends there had somehow made Micah shut down, go into self-defense mode. Jenny had told her that she'd never seen Micah happier than he was with Kelly. But since their weekend away, he'd drawn more into himself. It was nothing overt, but she *felt* the distance he was slamming down between them, and she had no idea how to get past it.

Yes, this had all started as a lie to make her grandmother feel better, but it had become so much more for Kelly. And maybe, she told herself, this was Karma's way of punishing her for the lie. Make her feel. Make her want. Then deny her. But even if it was, she told herself, she still had three months with Micah and she wouldn't let him leave her emotionally before he actually left.

Ruefully, Kelly admitted, "I can't bring myself to take the necklace off. It's like as long as I wear it, Micah's mine."

"Oh, sweetie, you've got it bad, don't you?"

"I love him." Her eyes went wide and she gasped a little before saying, "Oh, God. I love Micah." Kelly slapped both hands to her stomach as if she were going to be sick. "How could I do this?"

"Are you kidding?" Terry demanded. "Have you *looked* at him lately? It's a wonder it took you this long to fall for him. And that's not even counting the jewelry and the great sex."

Kelly laughed, but it sounded a little hysterical, even to her. She hadn't meant to fall in love, and she knew all too well that Micah would be horrified if she confessed what she felt for him. Heck, he'd probably be nothing more than a blur on his way out the door if he thought she was in love with him.

This had just slipped up on her. She hadn't meant to love him. And it wasn't the luxury vacations. Or the necklace. Or the sex—okay, maybe the sex was part of it. But she'd fallen in love with the *man*.

The man who could look so surprised when she didn't react the way he expected. The man who helped her with her haunted maze. The man who stood with a little boy so he could say good-night to his pumpkin.

"Oh, God," she whispered again. "This isn't good."

"Honey," Terry reached for her hand and squeezed it. "Maybe he loves you, too."

"Even if he did, he probably wouldn't tell me." Kelly shook her head. He'd been pretty clear, hadn't he? One engagement in his past and no desire for another. She could still hear him… *No wife. No girl-friend. No interest.* She closed her eyes and took a breath to try to steady herself. It didn't work.

"This wasn't supposed to be about love, Terry," she said, and was talking to herself as much as her friend. "This was just…"

"An affair?" Terry shook her head. "You're just not the affair kind of person, sweetie. This was *always* going to end up with you in love."

"You might have warned me," Kelly said miserably.

"You wouldn't have listened," Terry assured her and carried the cookie sheet to the oven. She slid it inside, set the timer and came back again. "You might be upset over nothing. I've seen you guys together and he does feel something for you, Kelly.

If it's not love, it's close. So, maybe he won't leave when his time here is done."

"I want to think that, but I can't." Kelly shook her head firmly. She'd already set herself up to have her heart broken. She wouldn't make it harder by holding on to the hope that things would change. "If I believe he'll stay, when he does eventually leave it'll only be worse on me."

"You could *try* to keep him here."

"No." Kelly had some pride, after all. She took another breath, squared her shoulders and lifted her chin. "If I had to *make* him stay then it wouldn't be worth it, would it?"

Terry sighed. "I hate when you're rational."

Kelly laughed sadly. "Thanks. Me, too." She finished off her latte. "He's going to leave, and I'll have to deal with that when it happens. For right now though, he's here. And I've got to go. Micah went to the university library today to do some research—"

"He's never heard of the internet?" Terry asked.

"He's a writer," Kelly said, with a sad smile. "He likes books. Anyway, I want to beat him home because I'm making dinner."

"I thought you said you loved him," Terry quipped.

"I'm not that bad," Kelly argued, though she could admit that she wasn't the best cook in the world, no one had died from eating what she made.

"Right." Terry turned and headed to the cooling racks. "Why don't I send some cookies home with you and then at least you'll have dessert."

"You're the best."

"So I keep telling Jimmy," Terry said with a wink.

The drive home only took a few minutes, but even at that, her faithful truck wheezed and coughed like an old man forced to run when all he wanted was a nap. Kelly sighed a little, knowing she'd be buying a new one soon.

Micah's car wasn't in the driveway, so Kelly took that as a good sign. She wasn't completely ready to face him yet. The whole *I'm in love* revelation had hit her hard and she needed a bit more time to deal with it.

Grabbing the grocery bags from the passenger seat, she headed into the kitchen through the back door. She had steaks, potatoes for baking, a salad and now the world's best cookies. After she put everything away, she opened a bottle of wine so it could breathe. Because, boy, she needed a glass of wine. Or two. Maybe it would help her settle.

She'd been married, been in love and, yet, this feeling she had for Micah was so huge it felt as if she might drown in it. And she couldn't tell him. Kelly had absolutely no desire to hand him her heart only to have him hand it right back.

She looked around the familiar kitchen as if she were lost and looking for a signpost to guide her home. Micah had stormed into her life with the promise to leave again in six months. Now she was halfway through that timeline and Kelly knew that nothing in her life would be the same without him in it.

"Oh, stop it," she told herself, slapping both hands onto the cold granite counter. "You're feeling sorry for yourself. You're missing him even though he's not even gone yet. So cut it out already." Nodding, she reacted to the personal pep talk by tucking her feelings away. There'd be plenty of time to explore them all later. But for now… "Grab a shower, and put on something easy to take off."

Wow. She was thinking about sex. Again. And had been since… "Micah came into your life, that's when."

Her stomach swirled again as she headed for the stairs. Nerves? Anticipation? Worry? She frowned a little. "Please don't be getting sick, that's all. There's enough going on without that. Besides, it's almost Halloween and there's way too much to do."

Kelly climbed the stairs, walked down the hall, turned into the big bedroom and stopped dead. "Who are you?"

The completely naked stranger propped up against Kelly's pillows stared at her. "I'm Misty. Who're you? Where's Micah?"

Nine

"Micah?" Kelly stared blankly at the woman. Why was she naked? Why was she here? In *their* bed? And mostly Kelly's brain screamed, *Why are you just standing there talking to her? Why aren't you calling the police?* All very good questions. And still, Kelly started with, "How did you get in?"

"The doors weren't locked." Misty sat up higher in the big bed, clutching the duvet to her bare breasts. Thick black hair fell in tousled waves around her shoulders. She had too much makeup on her wide blue eyes and her lips had been slicked a bright red. As for the rest of her, Kelly didn't want to know.

"You need to get dressed and get out of my house." Kelly folded her arms across her chest and tapped the toe of her boot against the rug. She was hoping to look intimidating. If that didn't work, the sheriff was next.

"*Your* house?" The woman sniffed and settled back more comfortably against the bank of pillows. "Micah Hunter lives here and I don't know what you're trying to pull, but he won't be happy when he comes home to find you."

God, Micah would be home any minute, too. Good thing? Bad? Who could tell?

"How do you know Micah?" Kelly had to wonder at the woman's complete confidence. Was she a girlfriend Micah hadn't told Kelly about? An ex, maybe?

"He's my soul mate," Misty declared dramatically. "I knew it the first time I read his books. His words speak to my *heart*. He's been waiting for me to find him and he won't appreciate *you* being here and spoiling our reunion."

Kelly shook her head. "Reunion?"

"We've lived lifetimes together," Naked Misty intoned with another touch of drama. "In each incarnation, we struggle to find each other again. At last now, we can be together as we were meant."

Baffled, Kelly could only stare at the woman. She was clearly delusional and that might make her dangerous. And she was *naked*. What was going— and that's when the truth hit her.

Naked Misty had to be one of the crazed fans Micah had told her about. He'd said they tracked him down and sneaked into hotel rooms. Sneaking into an unlocked Victorian had to have been a snap. Kelly was now alone with a crazy person who might at any moment decide that Kelly was her competition. She had to get Misty out of the house and she wanted backup for that plan. Finally, she pulled her cell phone from her back pocket.

"I'm calling the police if you're not out of this house in the next minute."

"You can't make me leave." Misty pouted prettily. She probably practiced the look in a mirror. "I'm not going anywhere until I see Micah. He'll *want* to see me," she said, letting the duvet slip a little to display the tops of a pair of very large breasts.

Irritated, Kelly realized she was going to have to burn the sheets, the duvet…maybe the bed. First, however, she had to get rid of Naked Misty.

"Kelly?" Micah's voice came in a shout from downstairs. "Are you here?"

"Well, backup's arrived. It seems you're about to get your wish," Kelly told the woman who was still pouting and using one hand to further tousle her hair to make the best possible impression. Without taking her eyes off the woman, Kelly shouted, "I'm upstairs, Micah. Could you come up?"

The tone of her voice must have clued him in that something was wrong. Kelly heard him come upstairs at a dead run, and when he swung around the corner into the room, he stopped right behind her.

"What the hell?"

"Micah," Naked Misty cried, then sat up straight, threw her arms wide in welcome and let the duvet drop, displaying what had to be man-made breasts of monumental proportions.

Kelly slapped one hand across her eyes. "Oh, I didn't need to see those."

"Me, neither," Micah muttered.

"Who's *she*?" Naked Misty demanded with a finger point of accusation at Kelly.

Micah gritted his teeth, then gave Kelly an apologetic look before saying, "Kelly's my fiancée. Who the hell are you? No," he corrected. "Never mind. Doesn't matter."

"You're *engaged*?" Misty sputtered and still managed to sound outraged. Betrayed.

"Yeah," Kelly said, then pointedly used Misty's own words in retaliation. "His words speak to my heart."

"How can you be engaged to *her*?"

Insulted, Kelly countered, "Hey, at least *my* breasts are real."

Honestly, she might have laughed at this mess, but the situation was just too weird.

"That's it," Micah ordered, stepping past Kelly to stride to the bed. "Get up whoever you are—"

"Misty."

"Of course you are." He huffed out a breath. "Well, Misty, get out of my bed, get dressed and get out."

"But I *love* you."

"Oh, boy," Kelly murmured. She didn't know whether to feel sorry for Misty or Micah or all three of them.

"No, you don't love me." Micah glared down at the woman until Misty seemed to shrink into the covers.

Kelly's stomach churned. Yes, Misty was crazy and an intruder, but she'd told Micah she loved him and he'd brushed it off coldly. And she knew that he probably wouldn't accept her declaration any better.

His features were cold, tight, as he stalked across the bedroom, scooping up the woman's discarded clothes. He tossed them at her and Naked Misty's pout deepened.

"You're mean."

"Damn straight." He stood beside the bed, legs braced, arms folded across his broad chest, and gave Misty a look that singed even as it iced. "If you're not out of this house in two minutes flat, I'll have you arrested."

"But—"

"If you ever come back," he added, "I'll have you arrested."

Naked Misty was pulling on a shirt as quickly as she could, thankfully tucking away those humongous breasts. "I only wanted to tell you how I feel. I do *love* you."

Kelly was watching now and saw the miserable resignation on Micah's face, and she didn't know how to help. She felt sorry for Misty, but she felt sorrier for herself. Loving Micah was hard. Knowing he wouldn't want her to was even harder.

"You don't even know me." He moved out of the woman's way when she leaped out of the bed and dragged her jeans on. Once she was dressed, Micah gave her enough time to scoop up her shoes and grab her purse from a chair. Then he took her by the arm and steered her out of the room.

Kelly heard them taking the stairs, but she didn't wait for Micah to come back. The only way to get a handle on the strangest situation she'd ever been in was to return things to normal. She immediately began stripping the bed. When Micah returned, he helped her take the sheets and duvet off and put on fresh sheets. Through it all he was silent, but the expression on his face told Kelly he wasn't happy.

"Did Misty get away all right?"

"Yeah." He huffed out a breath. "What the hell kind of name is Misty?" He smoothed the sheet, still avoiding her gaze. Well, Kelly wanted things back to normal between them, too.

"This wasn't your fault, Micah." She pulled the top sheet taut and folded the top back.

"She only came here because of me," he said, reaching for a replacement duvet, this one brick red, and flipping it out to cover the mattress.

"Still doesn't make it your fault." Kelly stacked pillows in fresh cases against the headboard. "How did she even find you?"

"Easy enough." Scowling, he too tossed a few

pillows onto the bed. "Like I told you. Social media is everywhere. Someone in Banner probably put it out on Facebook or Twitter that I was here. That's enough to get every nut in the world moving." Shaking his head, he smoothed wrinkles that weren't there. "She shows up in town, talks to a few people, finds out where I am and bingo. Naked in my bed."

That was just beyond creepy. Living your life knowing there were thousands of would-be stalkers out there, ready to hunt you down and barge into your life? Kelly shuddered. "I don't know how you deal with this stuff all the time."

"It's why I don't stay anywhere for very long," he said, walking around the end of the bed to come to her side. "And now that one has found me, others will be coming too. I can't stay, Kelly."

Panic blossomed in the center of her chest and sent out tendrils of ice that wrapped around her heart and squeezed. This was what she'd been feeling since their holiday in California. If Naked Misty hadn't shown up, it would have been something else. For whatever reason, Micah wanted to get away from Banner. From Kelly. "But…you haven't finished your book yet."

"I'm close though," he said. "I can finish it somewhere else."

She was losing him. Standing right in front of him and he was slipping away. "Why should you have to move out because of a crazy person?"

He sighed, dropped both hands onto her shoulders and met her eyes squarely. "It's not just her. Things have gotten…complicated between us, and I think it'd be easier if I left early."

"Easier? On who?"

"On both of us," he said, and stepped back. "Better to stop this before things get more tangled up."

But she wanted those three months. She wanted Micah here for the first snow, for Christmas. For New Year's Eve. She wanted him here *always*.

"Micah—" She broke off because anything she said now would sound like begging him to stay and she couldn't bring herself to do it. Couldn't make herself say *I love you*, either. He wouldn't believe her any more than he had Misty. Or, worse, he *would* believe her and feel sorry for her, and she refused to put herself in the position of having to accept either reaction.

"It's the best way, Kelly." His gaze locked with hers, and though she tried to read what he was feeling, thinking, it was as if he'd erected a barrier across his eyes to keep her out.

"Halloween's in a few days," he said. "I'll stay for that, okay? I'd like to see the kids go through that maze after spending so much time building the damn thing…"

A few days. That was all she had with him. So she'd take it and never let him know what it cost her to stay quiet. To let him go without asking him to stay.

"I'd like that, too," she said, and forced a smile that felt brittle and cold. "Where will you go?"

"I don't know," he admitted, stuffing his hands into his jeans pockets. "There's a hotel in Hawaii I like. Maybe I'll go there for a few months."

"Hawaii." Well, that couldn't be farther from Utah, could it? He was so anxious to be apart from her, he was sticking an ocean between them. Couldn't be clearer than that. "Okay, then."

He reached for her again but let his hand fall before he touched her, and that, Kelly thought, was so sad it nearly broke her heart.

"It's best this way, Kelly."

"Probably," she said, agreeing with him if only to see a flicker of surprise flash across his face. "Don't worry about me, Micah. I was good before you got here and I'll be fine when you leave." She wondered idly if her tongue would simply rot and fall out of her head on the strength of those lies. She picked up the dirty sheets and the duvet and held them to her like a shield. "I'll just go start the washing."

Kelly felt his gaze on her as she left the room, so she didn't look back. There was only so much she was willing to put herself through.

The morning of Halloween, Kelly had the black lights up and ready, the CD of haunted house noises—growls, moans, chains rattling and a great witch's cackle—loaded up and a mountain of candy for all of the trick-or-treaters.

She also had the same unhappy stomach she'd been dealing with for days. She wasn't worse, but she wasn't getting better, either. Which was why she'd made a quick trip to the drugstore. Not being a complete idiot, she didn't go to the mom-and-pop shop in Banner, instead driving down to Ogden to shop anonymously. One thing Kelly didn't need was the gossips in town speculating on if she was pregnant or not before she knew herself. At that thought, her stomach did another quick spin.

Micah was in his office typing away—pretty much where he'd been since Naked Misty had crashed into their lives uninvited, precipitating his announcement that he was leaving early.

The only time Kelly saw him lately was at night in bed. And though he might be trying to keep distance between them during the day, in the darkness Micah turned to her. Sex was just as staggering, but shadowed now with a thread of sorrow that neither of them wanted to talk about.

Kelly wanted to be with him as much as she could, but at the same time, whenever they came together, another tiny piece of her heart broke off and shattered at her feet. Seconds, minutes, hours were ticking away. All of her life she'd loved Halloween, and now for the first time, she hated it. Because he'd be leaving in the morning and Kelly was already dreading it.

She looked into the mirror over the bathroom sink and saw the misery in her own eyes. Her face was paler than usual, her freckles standing out like gold dust on vanilla ice cream. Kelly lifted her fingers to touch the cold surface of Micah's emerald as it shone brightly in the overhead light.

The tick of her kitchen timer sounded like a tiny heartbeat in the bathroom. *Tiny heartbeat.* Was it possible? Was she pregnant? And if she was, what then? When the buzzer sounded, letting her know the three minutes were up, Kelly shut down the timer, picked up the early-pregnancy-test stick and held her breath, still unsure what she was hoping for.

"A plus sign." She released that breath and giddily took another one. "Plus sign means *pregnant.*" She laughed and suddenly she knew exactly how she felt about this. Kelly grinned at her reflection. All of her doubts and worries disappeared, washed away by a wave of pure joy. "You don't have the flu. You have a *baby. Micah's baby.*"

She couldn't stop smiling. The woman in the mirror looked like a fool, standing there with that wide grin on her face, but Kelly didn't mind. This was… amazing. The most amazing thing that had ever happened to her. When Sean died, Kelly had never intended to remarry, so she'd had to accept that she'd never have children. And that was painful.

Then along came Micah, who swept her off her feet and into a tangle of emotions that had left her reeling right from the first time he'd kissed her. The misery of the last few days, pretending she was all right with him leaving just slid off her shoulders.

He was leaving, but he had also given her a gift. A wonderful gift. When Micah was gone, she'd still have a part of him with her. Always. She wouldn't be alone. She'd have her child and the memories of the man who'd given that child to her.

"I have to tell him," she said aloud, and looked down at the pregnancy test stick again as if to reassure herself that this was really happening. *It was.* Even though Micah was leaving, he had a right to know about his child. Her feelings were her own, but this baby, they shared.

Still smiling, she laid one hand over her belly in a protective gesture. "We'll be okay, you know. Just you and me, we'll be good."

Steeling herself, she nodded at her reflection, feeling new strength and determination fill her. When Micah left, her heart would be crushed. But she would have her baby to look after now and that was enough to keep her strong. "I'll tell him tonight. When Halloween's over. I'll tell him. And then I'll let him go."

Halloween was a rush of noise, laughter, shrieks and a seemingly never-ending stream of children. Micah had never done Halloween as a foster kid. And as an adult, he'd kept his distance from kids on general principle, so this holiday had never made much of an impact on him. Until celebrating it with Kelly.

Up and down the block, porch lights were on

and pumpkins glowed. Even the two nosy sisters, Margie and Sally, were across the street sitting on their front porch. They were bundled up against the cold and sipping tea, but they clearly wanted to watch all the kids.

The pumpkins Micah had taken Kelly to buy on their first ride together were carved into faces and shining with glow sticks inside them. Orange lights were stretched out along the porch railing. Black crepe paper fluttered from the gingerbread trim on the house and twisted in the wind. Polyester spiderwebs were strung out everywhere, and ghosts were suspended from the big oak tree out front.

Kelly was dressed up, of course, as her idea of a farmer, in overalls, a long-sleeved plaid shirt and work boots. Her hair was in pigtails and the emerald peeked out from behind the collar of her shirt. From the porch Micah handed out candy to those who made it through the haunted maze. Kelly had stationed herself in front of the maze to walk the little kids through personally so they wouldn't be scared. Cries of "Trick or treat!" rang out up and down the block. Parents kept stopping to congratulate him on his engagement, and Micah had to go along with the lies because he'd promised.

He wondered, though, what all of these people would think of him tomorrow when he left town, supposedly walking out on Kelly? He frowned. Good thing he didn't care.

Passing out candy like it was about to be banned,

Micah glanced around the yard and knew he was right to leave early. This wasn't his home. The sooner he got to a nice anonymous hotel the better. For everyone. Hell, he was handing out *candy*. He was carving pumpkins, for God's sake. Too much was changing and he didn't like it.

Even the tone of the book he'd been working on had changed. As if Kelly and what he'd found here with her had invaded even his fictional world. His heroine was now stronger, sexier, funnier than before. She stood up for herself and drove the hero as crazy as Kelly made Micah. Life was definitely imitating art. Or more the other way around.

"Micah!" A small hand tugged at the hem of Micah's coat, splintering his thoughts, which was just as well, since he had at least three hundred pounds of candy to give out.

Jacob, dressed like a lion, stared up at him. His lion's mane was yellow yarn and his nose had been colored black to match the whiskers drawn across his cheeks. "Are you scared cuz I'm a lion?"

"You bet." No point in dampening the excitement in the boy's eyes just because Micah was in a crap mood. "You make a good one."

"I can roar."

"I believe you."

"And you can come see my pumpkin all lit up, can't you? I put a happy face on it, but Daddy cut it cuz I'm too little to hold the knife."

"I will later," Micah said, wondering how he and

this little boy had become friends. "Don't you have to go with your brothers to get more candy?"

"Yeah, and I can have lots my dad says even though Mommy says no cuz daddies are the boss when Mom's not looking my dad says and Mommy laughed at him but said okay."

Micah blinked. That was a lot of words for one sentence. He wondered what the kid would be like next year. Or the year after. The kid would grow up in this town, play football, fall in love, get married and start the whole cycle over again. But Micah wouldn't be there to see any of it. Soon Jacob would forget all about a friend named Micah. And wasn't that irritating? "No, it's not."

"What?"

He looked down at the tiny lion. "Nothing, Jacob. Go on. Find your brothers. Have fun."

"Okay!"

As he ran off, Micah looked around and realized that he didn't belong there. He wasn't a part of this town. He could pretend to be. But the truth was he didn't belong anywhere and that's how he liked it. Who the hell else could just pick up and take off for Hawaii at a moment's notice? He was damn lucky living just the way he wanted to, answering to no one. He liked his life just fine and it was time to get back to it.

Several minutes later, he saw Jacob's parents rush up to Kelly, talking fast, looking all around frantically. Something was wrong. Micah left the candy bowl on the porch and took the steps down through the crowd. "What's going on?"

Kelly looked at him, worry etched into her features. "Jacob's missing."

He snorted. "No, he's not. He was just here a few minutes ago."

Jacob's mother, Nora, shook her head. "Jonas saw Jacob run into the woods. He was following a deer and Jonas ran to get us instead of going in after him."

"It was the right thing to do," her husband said. "Or they'd both be lost. You stay here, Nora, in case he finds his way out on his own. I've got my cell. Call me if you see him." Then he looked at Kelly, Micah and a few of the other adults. "If we split up, we should be able to find him fast."

Kelly pulled her cell phone out of her overalls, hit the flashlight app and looked up at Micah. "He's only three."

Micah was already headed to the woods, fighting a hard, cold knot that had settled in his gut. "We'll find him."

The woods were thick and dark and filled with the kind of shadows that lived in Micah's imagination. It was the perfect setting for murder. Wisps of fog, moonlight trickling through bare branches of trees, the rustle of dead leaves on the ground and the quick, scuttling noise of something rushing through them. It was as if he'd written the scene himself. But it wasn't so good for a lost little boy. They moved as quickly as they could, their flashlights bobbing and dancing in the darkness. Roots jutted from the ground and Kelly tripped more than once as they hurried through the trees.

Kelly called for Jacob over and over, but there was no answer. The flashlight beams looked eerie, shining past the skeletons of trees to get lost in the pines. *Where the hell was he? He hadn't had enough time to go far.* Micah fought down his own sense of frustration and worry, but they came rushing back up. Anything could happen to a kid that size. His writer's mind listed every possibility and each was worse than the last.

He shouldn't have let the kid wander off to find his brothers alone.

"God," Kelly murmured, turning in a slow circle. "Where is he?"

"Hiding? Chasing the deer?" Micah strained his eyes, looking from right to left. "Who the hell knows?"

From a distance came the calls of the others searching for the little boy, and their flashlights looked like ghosts moving through the shadows. Micah had to wonder why Jacob wasn't answering. Was he hurt? God. Unconscious? In the next instant, Micah thought he heard something so he pulled Kelly to a stop.

"Listen. There it is again." He whipped his head around. "Over there."

"Jacob?" Micah shouted and this time he was sure he heard the little boy yell, "I'm lost."

"Thank God." Kelly ran right behind him and in seconds they'd found him. Jacob was scared and cold and his sneaker was caught under a tree root.

"The deer ran away," he said as if that explained everything.

Micah's heart squeezed painfully. "The deer doesn't matter. You okay, buddy? Are you hurt?"

"No," he said, "I'm stuck. And I'm cold. And I spilled my candy."

Kelly's flashlight caught his overturned pumpkin basket with the candy bars scattered around it. She quickly scooped them all up.

"See? Kelly's got your stuff and we can fix the rest," Micah said. "Kelly, call Jacob's dad. Tell him he's okay."

"Already on it," she said, and he heard her talking.

"Am I in trouble?" Jacob rubbed his eyes, smearing his whiskers.

Once he freed the boy's foot, Micah picked him up. "I don't think so. Your parents are probably going to be too happy to see you to be mad."

"Okay, good. I still need to get more candy." Jacob wrapped his arms around Micah's neck. "When we get back you wanna see my pumpkin?"

Kelly laughed. Micah caught her eye and grinned. Kids were damn resilient. More so than the adults they scared the life out of. He took a breath and slowly released it. With the boy's arms around his shoulders and Kelly smiling at him, Micah knew he'd become too attached. Not just to Kelly, but to this place. Even this little boy.

And as they left the shadows and stepped into the light again, Micah knew he'd stayed too long. He had to leave. While he still could.

A part of Kelly wanted to do just what he was sure she would. Cry, ask him to stay. But none of that would help. Just as she'd told Terry, if she had to force him to be with her, then what they had wasn't worth having.

She wouldn't tell him she loved him. He should know that already from the way they were together—and if he didn't, it was because he didn't *want* to know. So Kelly would keep her feelings to herself and remain perfectly rational.

Too bad it did nothing for the hole opening up in the center of her chest.

"I called for the jet," Micah said, stuffing his folded clothes into a huge black duffel. His suits were already in a garment bag laid out on the bed. Their bed.

"So you'll be in Hawaii late tonight."

"Or early in the morning, yeah." He zipped the bag closed, straightened up and faced her. His features were unreadable, his eyes shadowed. "Look, I know I said I was leaving tomorrow, but there's no reason to wait and I thought it would be easier this way."

Nothing about this was easy, but Kelly smiled.

She would get through this. "Did you get everything?"

He glanced around the room, "Yeah. I did. Kelly…"

God, she didn't want him to say he was sorry. Didn't want to see sympathy in his eyes or hear it in his voice. She cut him off with the one sure way she knew to make him stop talking. "Before you go, I've got something you need to see."

His eyes narrowed on her suspiciously. "What is it?"

Kelly took a breath, pulled the test stick from her pocket and handed it to him. Still confused, he stared at her for another second or two, then his gaze dropped to the stick. "Is this—" He looked into her eyes. "You're pregnant?"

"I am. Thought I was getting sick, but no."

"We used protection."

"Apparently latex just isn't what it used to be." It was hard to smile, but she did it. Hard to keep her spirits up, but she was determined. Kelly took a step toward him. "Micah, I just thought you had a right to know about the baby. I—"

"How long have you known?"

"Since this morning."

"And you waited until I'm all packed and ready to go before you drop it on me?"

"Well," she said, her temper beginning to rise, "I didn't know you were leaving tonight, did I? Sprung that one on me."

"What's that supposed to mean?"

"Oh, come on, Micah." Her vow to remain rational was slowly unraveling. But then, she told herself, temper wasn't pitiful. "You know exactly what I mean. You wanted to catch me off guard so I wouldn't have time to plead with you not to go."

He stiffened. "That's not—"

"Relax. I'm not asking you to stay, Micah. Go ahead. Leave. I know you have to, or at least that you think you have to, which pretty much amounts to the same thing anyway. So go. I'm fine."

"You're pregnant," he reminded her.

Kelly laid both hands on her belly and for the first time that night gave him a real smile. "And will be, whether you're here or not. I'm *happy* about the baby. This is a gift, Micah. The best one you could have given me."

"A gift." He shook his head and paced the room, occasionally glancing down at the stick he still held. "Happy. My God, you and this place…"

"What're you talking about?" Now it was her turn to be confused, but she didn't like the cornered anger snapping in his eyes.

He shoved one hand through his hair. "You don't even see it, do you?" Muttering now, he said, "I told myself earlier that I didn't belong here and I know why. But you just don't get it."

"I don't appreciate being talked down to," Kelly snapped. "So if you've got something to say, just say it."

"You're pregnant and you're *happy* about it, even though I'm walking out and leaving you alone to deal with it."

"That's a bad thing? Micah—"

"You live in a land of kids and dogs." He choked out a short laugh and shook his head as if even he couldn't believe all of this. "You paint pictures on windows, carve pumpkins." He threw up his hands. "You have nosy neighbors, deer in your garden and ghosts hanging from your tree, and none of that has anything to do with the real world. With the world I live in."

He was simmering. She could see frustration and anger rippling off him in waves and Kelly responded to it. If he was leaving, let them at least have truth between them when he did.

"Which world is that, Micah?" When he didn't speak, she prompted, "Go ahead. You're clearly on a roll. Tell me all about how little I know about reality."

He laughed, but there was no humor in the sound. Tossing the test stick onto the bed, he stalked to her side. "You want reality?" He looked down into her eyes and said, "I grew up in foster homes. My mother walked out when I was six and I never saw her again. I didn't have a damn friend until I met Sam in the navy, because I never stayed anywhere long enough to make one." His gaze bored into hers. "My world is hard and cruel. I don't have the slightest clue how to live in a land where everything is rosy all the damn time."

He was breathing fast, his eyes flashing, but he had nothing on Kelly. She could feel her temper building inside her like a cresting wave, and like a surfer at the beach, she jumped on board and rode it.

"Rosy?" Insult stained her tone as she poked him in the chest with her index finger. "You think my world is some cozy little space? That my life is perfect? My parents died when I was little and I came here to live when I was twelve. Then my grandfather died. My *husband* died. And my best friend's husband is in danger every day he's deployed."

He swiped one hand across his face. "God, Kelly…"

"Not finished," she said, tipping her head back to glare at him. "Life happens, Micah. Even in *rosy* little towns. People die. Three-year-olds get lost in the woods. And men who don't know any better walk away."

His jaw was tight and turmoil churned in his eyes. "Damn it, Kelly, I wasn't thinking."

She heard the contrition in his voice, but she couldn't let go of her anger. If she did, the pain would slide in and that might just finish her off. Thank God she hadn't told him she loved him— that would have been the capper to this whole mess.

"You're the one who doesn't get it, Micah," she said. "Bad things happen. You just have to keep going."

"Or you stop," he countered. "And back away."
Micah shook his head. "I don't know how to do this,
Kelly. You. This town. A *baby*, for God's sake. Trust
me when I say I'm not the guy you think I am."

"No, Micah," she said, feeling sorrow swallow
the anger. "You're not the guy *you* think you are."

He snorted and shook his head. "Still surprising
me." He walked to the bed, picked up his bags and
stood there, staring at her. "Anything you need, call
me. You or the baby. You've got my cell number."

"I do," she said, lifting her chin and meeting his
gaze steadily. "But I won't need anything, Micah.
I don't want anything from you." All she wanted
was *him*. But she realized now she couldn't have
him. Her heart was breaking and that empty place
in her heart was spreading, opening like a black
hole, devouring everything in its path.

She felt hollowed out, and looking at him now
only made that worse. He was close enough to touch
and so far away she couldn't reach him.

"Goodbye, Kelly," he said, and, carrying his
bags, he walked past her.

She heard him on the stairs. Heard the front door
open and then close, and he was gone.

Dropping to the end of the bed, Kelly looked
around the empty room and listened to the silence.

Ten

By the following afternoon, Kelly had most of the Halloween decorations down and stacked to be put away. This chore used to depress her, since the anticipation and fun of the holiday was over for another year. But today she already felt as low as she could go.

"I still can't believe he left, knowing you're pregnant."

Kelly sighed. She'd told her best friend the whole story and somehow felt better the more outraged Terry became. But it had been an hour and she was still furious. "Terry, he was always going to leave, remember?"

"Yeah, but *pregnant* changes things."

"No, it doesn't."

"Plus," Terry added, "I can't believe you're pregnant before me. Jimmy's got his work cut out for him when he gets home."

Kelly laughed as Terry had meant her to. What did people without best friends do when the world exploded? Her mind wandered as she rolled up the orange twinkle lights from the porch and carefully stored them in a bag marked for Halloween.

She'd done a lot of thinking the night before—since God knows she hadn't gotten any sleep—and had come to the conclusion that she'd done the right thing. Kelly didn't want Micah to stay because of the baby. She wanted him to stay for *her.*

"If he had stayed because I'm pregnant," she told Terry, "sooner or later, he'd resent us both and *then* he'd leave." Shaking her head firmly, she said, "This way is better. Not great, but better."

"Okay, I get that, and I hate it when you're mature and I'm not," Terry said. "But I'd still feel better if Jimmy were here and I could tell him to go beat Micah up."

Kelly laughed, hugged her best friend and said, "It's the thought that counts."

Her cell phone rang and she cringed at the caller ID. Looking at Terry, she said, "It's Gran."

"Oh, boy." Shaking her head, Terry said, "Let's go inside. You can sit down and I'll make some tea."

As the phone continued to ring, Kelly mused,

"It's a shame I can't have wine because, boy, after this conversation, I'm going to need some."

Kelly wasn't looking forward to breaking this news to her grandmother, but she might as well get it over with. She followed Terry into the house and answered the phone. "Hi, Gran."

"Sweetie, I found the prettiest wedding dress—it would be perfect on you. I'm going to send you the picture, okay, and I don't want to interfere, but—"

Kelly sat down at the table and winced at Terry, already moving around the kitchen. Bracing herself, she interrupted her grandmother's flow. "Gran, wait. I've got something to tell you."

"What is it, dear? Oh, hold on. Linda's here, I'm putting you on speaker."

Great. Kelly sighed and winced again. "Well, the good news is, I'm pregnant!"

Terry frowned at her and mouthed, *Chicken*, as she wandered the kitchen making tea. Kelly set the phone on the table, hit speaker and her grandmother's and Aunt Linda's voices spilled into the room.

"Oh, a baby!"

"That's so wonderful," Linda cooed. "You know my Debbie keeps telling me she's going to one of those sperm banks, but she hasn't done it yet. You should talk to her, Kelly."

Terry laughed and once again, Kelly felt bad for her cousin Debbie. First an engagement and now a baby. She was putting a lot of pressure on Debbie and Tara.

"Oh, Micah must be so excited," Gran said.

"Yeah," Terry threw in. "He's thrilled."

Kelly scowled at her. *Not helping.*

"That's the thing, Gran," Kelly said quickly. "The bad news is that Micah and I broke up."

"What?" Twin shrieks carried all the way from Florida, and Kelly had the distinct feeling she might have heard the two women without the phone.

Terry set out some cookies and brewed tea while Kelly went through the whole thing for the second time that day. A half hour later, Gran and Aunt Linda were both fuming.

"I'll get Big Eddie to go out there and give that boy a punch in the nose."

"Oh, for heaven's sake, Linda," Gran said. "Big Eddie's seventy-five years old."

"He's tough, though," Linda insisted. "Spry, too and I have reason to know."

"Spry or not, you can't ask the man to fly somewhere just to punch someone, no matter how badly he deserves it," Gran snapped.

Terry set cups of tea on the table, then gave two thumbs-ups in approval.

"No one needs to beat anybody up," Kelly said, sipping her fresh cup of tea. "I had no idea my family was so violent. Terry already offered to have Jimmy do the honors."

"Terry's a good girl, I always said so."

"Thanks, Gran," Terry called out.

"What are you going to do about all of this, Kelly?" Gran asked.

"I'm gonna have a baby," she said, then added quickly, "and I'm going to be fine, Gran. I don't want you rushing home to take care of me."

"She's got me right here," Terry said.

"This just doesn't seem right, though," Gran mumbled. "You shouldn't be alone."

Kelly ate a cookie and thought about another one.

"Get a clue, Bella," Linda told her. "The girl doesn't want you there hovering. She's got things to do, to think about, isn't that right, Kelly?"

If she'd been closer, Kelly would have kissed her aunt. "Thanks, Aunt Linda. Honest, Gran, I'm fine. Micah's doing what he has to do and so am I."

"I don't like it," her grandmother said, then sighed. "But you're a grown woman, Kelly, and I'll respect your decisions."

Terry's eyes went wide in surprise and Kelly stared at the phone, stunned. "Really?"

"You'll figure it out, honey," Gran said.

"You will," Linda added. "And if you need us for anything, you call and say so. A great-grandchild's something to celebrate, like I keep telling Debbie."

"This one's mine," Gran pointed out.

"Oh, you can share," Linda said. "I'll share when Debbie finally comes through."

Terry was laughing and Kelly almost cried. She'd been hit by a couple of huge emotional jolts in the last twenty-four hours, but the bottom line was that she had her family. She wasn't alone. She just didn't have Micah.

And that was going to hurt for a long time.

For a solid week, Micah holed up in his penthouse suite. He couldn't work. Couldn't sleep. Had no interest in eating. He lived on coffee and sandwiches from room service he forced down. A deep, simmering fury was his only companion and even at that, he knew it was useless. Hell, *he* was the one who left. Why was he so damn mad?

The second week gone was no better, though anger shifted to worry and that made him furious, too. He hadn't wanted any of this. Hadn't asked to care. Didn't want to wonder if Kelly was all right. If the baby was okay. And it was November and that meant snow for her, and he started thinking about her broken-down truck and her riding around in it, and that drove him even crazier.

Micah wasn't used to this. Once he moved on from a place, he wiped it from his mind as if it didn't even exist anymore. He was always about the next place. He didn't do the past. He moved around on his own and liked it. He didn't *miss* people, so why the hell did he wake up every morning reaching for Kelly in that big empty bed?

"You Kelly Flynn?"

The burly man in a blue work shirt and khaki

slacks held a clipboard and looked at her through a pair of black-framed glasses.

"Yes, I am. Who're you?"

"I'm Joe Hackett. I'm here to deliver your truck?"

"My what?" Kelly stepped onto the porch of the cottage and looked out at the driveway. Parked behind her old faithful truck was a brand-new one. November sunlight made the chrome sparkle against the deep glossy red paint. It was bigger than her old one, with a shorter bed but a longer cab with a back seat bench. It was shiny. And new. And beautiful. Kelly loved it. But it couldn't be hers. "There must be some mistake."

"No mistake, lady," Joe said. "Sign here and she's all yours. Paid for free and clear including tax and license."

She looked from the truck to the clipboard and saw her name and address on the delivery sheet. So not a mistake. Which could mean only one thing. Micah had sent it.

He'd been gone two weeks. The longest two weeks of her life. And, suddenly, here he was. Okay, not *him*, but his presence, definitely. Tears filled her eyes and she had to blink frantically to clear her vision. What was she supposed to think about this? He leaves but buys her a new truck? Why would he do it?

"Lady? Um, just sign here so we can get going?" He was giving her the nervous look most men wore around crying women.

"Right. Okay." She scrawled her name on the bottom line and took the keys Joe handed over. As he and another guy left in a compact car, Kelly walked to her new truck. She ran her hand across the gleaming paint, then opened the driver's-side door and got in. The interior sparkled just as brightly as the outside. Leather seats. Seat warmers. Backup camera. Four-wheel drive. She laughed sadly. The truck had so many extras it could probably drive itself.

"Micah, why?" She sat back and stared through the windshield at the Victorian. Her fingers traced across the surface of the emerald she still wore, and she wondered where he was now and if he missed her as much as she missed him.

Micah hated the hotel. He felt like a rat in a box.

The penthouse suite was huge, and still he felt claustrophobic. He couldn't just step outside and feel a cold fall breeze. No, he'd have to take an elevator down thirty floors and cross a lobby just to get to the damn parking lot.

He didn't keep the doors to the terrace open because they let in the muffled roar of the city far below. He'd gotten so used to the quiet at Kelly's place that the noise seemed intrusive rather than comforting.

Three weeks now since he'd left Kelly, and the anger, the worry, the outrage had all boiled down into a knot of guilt, which made him mad all over again.

What the hell did he have to feel guilty about? She'd known going in that he wasn't going to stay. And if she'd wanted him to stay why didn't she say so?

No. Not Kelly. *I'm fine. I have the baby. We don't need anything from you.*

"Perfect. She doesn't need me. I don't need her. Then we're both happy. *Right?*" Was she driving that new truck? Had it snowed yet? Had she gotten the plow blade attached to the new truck? Was she out plowing people's roads and drives? Was she doing it alone?

God, he hated this room.

Pregnant.

She was carrying *his* kid, and what the hell was he supposed to do about that? If she'd wanted his help, she would have said so. But she didn't beg him not to leave. Hell, she hadn't even watched him go. What the hell was that about? Did she just not give a damn?

Irritation spiking, he grabbed his cell phone, hit the speed dial and waited for Sam to answer.

"Hi, Micah. What's up?"

What *wasn't* up? Micah hadn't talked to Sam since leaving Utah mainly because he just hadn't wanted to talk to anyone, really. Now he'd been alone with his own thoughts for too long and needed…something. He pushed one hand through his hair, walked to the open terrace doors and stared out at the ocean. The last time he'd had an ocean view, he'd been on a different terrace. With Kelly. And *that* memory would kill him if he started thinking about it. So he didn't.

"Kelly's pregnant." He hadn't meant to just say it, but it was as if the words had been waiting for a chance to jump out.

"That's great. Congratulations, man."

He scowled. "Yeah, thanks I guess. Kelly told me about the baby the night I left."

"You left? Where the hell are you?"

"Hawaii." Paradise, his ass. There was too much sunshine here. People were too damn cheerful.

"Why?"

"Because it was time to go." Micah scrubbed one hand across his jaw and remembered he hadn't shaved in a couple weeks. "I couldn't stay. Things were getting too—"

"Real?" Sam asked.

He frowned at the phone. "What's that supposed to mean?"

"It means that you've never lived an ordinary life, Micah. You went from your crap childhood to the navy to posh hotels."

Micah scowled into the wide mirror over the gas fireplace as he listened.

"You've never had a real woman, either. All those models and actresses? They weren't looking for anything more than you were—one night at a time." Sam paused. "Trust me when I say that has nothing to do with the real world."

God, hadn't he thrown practically the same accusation at Kelly that last night with her?

"What's your point?" God. *Points*. He rubbed his eyes tiredly. They felt like marbles in a bucket of sand.

"My point is—Kelly is *real*. What you had there mattered, Micah, whether you admit it or not, and I think it scared the crap out of you."

"I wasn't scared." He remembered telling little Jacob that everybody got scared sometimes. That included him, didn't it?

The realization was humbling.

"Sure you were," Sam said jovially. "Every guy is scared out of his mind when he meets the one woman who matters more than anything."

"I never said anything like that—"

"You didn't have to, Micah." He chuckled, which was damn irritating. "I've known you long enough to figure things out for myself. For example. When's the last time you left a hotel in the middle of a book?"

He blew out a breath. "Well…"

"Never, that's when," Sam told him. "You stay six months at every place you go. This time you bolt after three? Come on, Micah."

The man in the mirror looked confused. Worried. Was that it? Had he run from Kelly because she mattered? Because he was afraid? He turned away from the damn mirror because he couldn't stand to see the questions in his own eyes. "Look, I didn't call for advice. I just wanted you to know where I am."

"Great, but you get the advice anyway," Sam said. "Do yourself a favor and go back to Kelly. Throw yourself on her mercy and maybe she'll take your sorry ass back."

Micah glared at the room because it wasn't the Victorian. Because Kelly wasn't here with him. Because he was hundreds of miles away from her and he didn't know what she was doing. How she was feeling. "How the hell can I do that? What do I know about being somebody's father, for God's sake?"

"If nothing else," Sam said, "you know what *not* to do. And that's stay away from your own kid. You grew up without a father. That's what you want for your baby, too?"

Putting it like that gave Micah something to think about. He'd done to his kid exactly what his mother had done to him. "I'm no good at this stuff, Sam."

"Nobody is, Micah. We just figure it out as we go along."

"Well, that's comforting."

"Figure it out, Micah. Don't be an ass."

On that friendly piece of advice, Sam hung up, leaving Micah with too much to think about.

* * *

The first snow hit two days later, but it was a mild storm after warm days, so the snow wasn't sticking. Which meant Kelly didn't have to go out and clear any drives or private roads. Instead, she was cozy in the Victorian, enjoying the snap and hiss of the fireplace. She'd been staying in the cottage because she didn't want to torture herself with memories of Micah in the Victorian. But, with winter here, she wanted the fireplace, so she convinced herself that the only way to get past the pain of missing Micah was by facing it.

With a cup of tea, a book and the fire, the setting would have been perfect. If Micah were there.

The front door opened suddenly and Kelly's heart jolted. She jumped up, ran to the hall, and all of the air left her lungs as she stood there in shock staring at Micah. Snow dusted his shoulders and his hair. He dropped his duffel bag, slammed the front door and flipped the dead bolt. When he turned around and saw her, he scowled.

"Lock the damn door, Kelly. *Anybody* could just walk into the house."

She laughed shortly and seriously considered racing down the hall and throwing herself into his arms. It was only pride that kept her in place. "Anybody did."

"Very funny." Still scowling fiercely, he walked down the hall, took her arm and steered her into the living room.

"What're you doing, Micah?" She pulled her arm from his grip even though she wanted nothing more than to hold on to him. And she desperately wished she wasn't wearing her new flannel pajamas decorated with dancing pandas. "Why are you here?"

His gaze moved over her as if he were etching her image into his brain. Then he stepped back and stalked to the fireplace. Turning around to face her from a safe distance, he said, "You know, I thought I was doing the right thing."

"By leaving?"

"Yeah." He sighed heavily. Shaking his head, Micah stared down at the fire for a long minute before lifting his gaze to hers. "Kelly, I have no idea how to do *this*." He waved one hand to encompass the house, her, the baby and everything else that was so far out of his experience. "You know how I told you I was engaged once before? I said it didn't take?"

"Yes." She'd wondered about that woman in his past.

"I ended it because I didn't care enough. I figured I was incapable of caring enough," he ground out, and she could see that the words were costing him. "Then I met you."

Heat began to melt the ice that had been around her heart for weeks. Hope rose up in her chest, and Kelly clung to it but kept quiet, wanting him to go on. To say it all.

He threw his hands high, then snorted. "Hell,

I've never known anyone like you. You made me nuts. Made me feel things I never have. Want things I never wanted."

"Thanks."

Micah laughed and shook his head. "See? Like that. You surprise me all the damn time, Kelly. I never know where I'm standing with you and, turns out, I like it."

"You do?"

"Gotta have it," he admitted, and swallowed hard. He took a step toward her, then stopped. "The last three weeks I've been so bored I thought I was losing my mind. I was at a hotel I'd been in before and this time, I hated it. Hated that it was small and there was no damn yard with deer and kids running through it. Hated that it was so damn noisy—but the wrong kind of noise, you know?"

"No," she admitted, smiling. "What are you saying, Micah?"

"I'm saying—all I could think about was you. And the baby. And this place. But mostly *you.*"

Tears were coming and she couldn't stop them this time. Didn't even try. They rolled unheeded down her cheeks as Kelly kept her gaze fixed on the only man in the world for her.

"You love me," he said, pointing a finger at her.

"Do I?" she said, and her smile widened.

"Damn right you do." Micah started walking—well, *stalking* the perimeter of the room. "A woman like you...love shows. Not just the sex, though that was great, for sure."

"It was."

"But you were there. Every day. You laughed with me. You cooked with me." He glared at her. "Yet, when I tell you I'm leaving, you just say, have a nice trip and by the way I'm pregnant."

Kelly flushed. "Well, that's not exactly—"

"Basically," he snapped. "That was it. And I finally started wondering why you hadn't told me that you love me. Why didn't you use the baby as a lever to keep me here? Why didn't you beg me to stay?"

She stiffened and tried to look as dignified as possible in her panda pj's. "I don't beg."

"No," he said thoughtfully, his gaze locked with hers. "You wouldn't. Just like you wouldn't coerce me to stay. You were way sneakier than that."

"Me?" Now Kelly laughed. "I am *not* sneaky."

"This time you were," he said, and walked across the room to her. "You let me go, knowing I'd be miserable without you. You didn't say you loved me because you knew I'd wonder about that. And you didn't tell me I loved you because you wanted me to figure it out for myself. You wanted me to be away long enough to realize I was being a damn fool."

"That was clever of me." Or would have been if she'd actually planned it. She swayed, bit her bottom lip and held her breath. "And did you? Figure it all out?"

"I'm here, aren't I?" He blew out a breath,

grabbed her and pulled her in close to him. Wrapping his arms around her, he rested his chin on top of her head and whispered, "You feel so good. This—*us*—is so good. I love you, Kelly. Didn't know I *could* love. But maybe I was only waiting to find you."

"Oh, Micah…" She held on to him, nestled her head against his chest and listened to the steady beat of his heart. It was as if every one of her dreams was coming true. The last three weeks had been so painful. Now there was so much joy she felt as if she were overflowing. "I love you, too."

"I know."

She laughed and tipped her head back to stare at him. "Sure of yourself, are you?"

"I am now," he admitted. "And I'm sure about this, too. You're going to have to marry me for real. It's the only answer. I have to be here in this big old house with you. I need to be with you at Christmas. I have to help you run for mayor. And next year, Jacob and I will help you plant the pumpkin patch. I want to meet Jimmy—I think he and I can be friends when we bond over our crazy women."

Kelly's heart was flying. "I'll have to give you a point for that crazy proposal."

He grinned. "Not a proposal. Just an acceptance of your earlier proposal. Remember?"

"You're right. So, no points."

"No more points at all," he said softly. "Say yes and we *both* win."

Kelly laughed, delighted with him, with everything. "Of course, yes."

"Good." He nodded as if checking things off a mental list. "That's settled. I've got to ride with you when you start plowing and—" He stopped. "Did you like the truck?"

She laughed again, a little wildly, but she didn't care. "I love it, you crazy man."

"Huh. You plow snow, but I'm crazy." He shook his head and stared down at her with hope and relief and *love* shining in his eyes.

"I never should have left, Kelly," he whispered, "but in a way I guess I had to, because I never learned how to *stay*. But I want to stay now, Kelly. With you. With our kids…"

"Kids?" she asked hopefully. "Plural?"

He grinned. "It's a big house. We should do our best to fill it."

God, this was everything Kelly had ever wanted, and more. The firelight threw dancing shadows across Micah's face, making his eyes shine with hope and promise and love. "I love you so much, Micah. I'm so glad you came home."

He cupped her face in his palms and kissed her tenderly. "The only home I ever want is wherever you are. For the first and last time in my life, I'm in love. And I never want to lose it."

"You won't," she promised. "*We* won't."

He blew out a breath and said, "Damn straight we won't. Now. For part two of my brilliant plan."

"You had a plan?"

"Still do and I think you'll like it," he said, sweeping her up in his arms, surprising a laugh out of her. He sat down in one of the overstuffed chairs and held her on his lap. He frowned at her pajamas. "What are those? Dogs?"

"Pandas."

"Sure. Why not?" Shaking his head, he said, "I'm thinking we hire a jet and fly to Florida tomorrow—"

"Tomorrow?"

"—pick up your grandmother and your aunt, and then all of us go to New York for a week. Maybe the Ritz-Carlton. I think they'd like that place."

"What?"

He shrugged. "I've never had a family before. I'd like to get to know them. Have them meet Sam and Jenny and the kids, because they're as close to family as I've ever known. And while we're there, your grandmother can help you pick out that ring we talked about."

"Oh, Micah!" Many more surprises and her head would simply spin right off her shoulders. She threw her arms around his neck and kissed him hard and fast. Then something occurred to her. "We'd better call first, though."

"Why?"

"I told Gran and Aunt Linda that we broke up and they were arranging for one of the seniors to fly out and punch you in the nose."

"More surprises," Micah said, grinning. "I'll risk it if you will."

"Absolutely," she said.

"I love you, Kelly Flynn."

"I love you, Micah Hunter," she said, melting against him. As he bent his head to claim another kiss, Kelly whispered, "Welcome home."

* * * * *

*If you loved this sexy, emotion-filled romance
from* USA TODAY *bestselling author
Maureen Child,
pick up these other titles!*

*THE TEMPORARY MRS. KING
HER RETURN TO KING'S BED
DOUBLE THE TROUBLE
THE COWBOY'S PRIDE AND JOY
THE BABY INHERITANCE*

Available now from Harlequin Desire!

***

*If you're on Twitter, tell us what you think of
Harlequin Desire! #harlequindesire.*

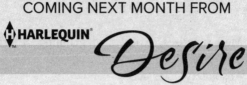
#2551 THE TEXAN TAKES A WIFE

Texas Cattleman's Club: Blackmail • by Charlene Sands

Erin Sinclair's one-night stand with sexy cowboy Daniel Hunt is just what she needs. But when she offers to help out a friend and ends up working with someone *very* familiar, she'll soon learn just how determined a cowboy can be!

#2552 TWINS FOR THE BILLIONAIRE

Billionaires and Babies • by Sarah M. Anderson

Real estate mogul Eric Jenner is more than willing to work with his childhood friend Sofia. The single mom needs to provide for her adorable twins. But will combining business and pleasure lead to love...or to heartbreak?

#2553 LITTLE SECRETS: HOLIDAY BABY BOMBSHELL

by Karen Booth

Hotel heiress Charlotte Locke vows to best her commitmentphobic ex Michael Kelly in a business battle. But when he learns she's having his child, he'll have to convince her he'll do right by their child—and her heart—or risk losing her forever.

#2554 EXPECTING A LONE STAR HEIR

Texas Promises • by Sara Orwig

To fulfill a promise, US Army Ranger Mike Moretti goes home to Texas to work on the Warner ranch. His attraction to the owner—his friend's widow—is a temptation he can't resist, and then she announces a little surprise...

#2555 TWELVE NIGHTS OF TEMPTATION

Whiskey Bay Brides • by Barbara Dunlop

Mechanic Tasha Lowell is not his type. She's supposed to be repairing CEO Matt Emerson's yacht, not getting under his skin. But when a charity-ball makeover reveals the sensuous woman underneath the baggy clothes, Matt knows he must have her...

#2556 WRANGLING THE RICH RANCHER

Sons of Country • by Sheri WhiteFeather

When reclusive rancher Matt Clark, the troubled son of a famous country singer, confronts the spunky Libby Penn about her biography of his estranged father, anger and distrust might be replaced with something a whole lot more dangerous to his heart...

SPECIAL EXCERPT FROM

HARLEQUIN™

Desire

*To fulfill a promise, US Army Ranger Mike Moretti
goes home to Texas to work on the Warner ranch.
His attraction to the owner—his friend's widow—is a
temptation he can't resist, and then she announces a
little surprise...*

Read on for a sneak peek of
EXPECTING A LONE STAR HEIR
by USA TODAY *bestselling author Sara Orwig,
the first book in her new **TEXAS PROMISES** series.*

As Mike stepped out of the car, his gaze ran over the
sprawling gray stone mansion that looked as if it should
be in an exclusive Dallas suburb instead of sitting on a
mesquite-covered prairie.

After running his fingers through his wavy ebony hair,
Mike put on his broad-brimmed black Stetson. As he strode
to the front door, he realized he had felt less reluctance
walking through minefields in Afghanistan. He crossed the
wide porch that held steel-and-glass furniture with colorful
cushions, pots of greenery and fresh flowers. He listened
to the door chimes and in seconds, the ten-foot intricately
carved wooden door swung open.

He faced an actual butler.

"I'm Mike Moretti. I have an appointment with
Mrs. Warner."

"Ah, yes, we're expecting you. Come in. I'm Henry, sir.
If you'll wait here, sir, I'll tell Mrs. Warner you've arrived."

HDEXP1017

"Thank you," Mike replied, nodding at the butler, who turned and disappeared into a room off the hall.

Henry reappeared. "If you'll come with me, sir, Mrs. Warner is in the study." Mike followed him until Henry stopped at an open door. "Mrs. Warner, this is Mike Moretti."

"Come in, Mr. Moretti," she said, smiling as she walked toward him.

He entered a room filled with floor-to-ceiling shelves of leather-bound books. After the first glance, he forgot his surroundings and focused solely on the woman approaching him.

Mike had seen his best friend Thane's pictures of his wife—one in his billfold, one he carried in his duffel bag. Mike knew from those pictures that she was pretty. But those pictures hadn't done her justice because in real life, Vivian Warner was a downright beauty. She had big blue eyes, shoulder-length blond hair, flawless peaches-and-cream complexion and full rosy lips. The bulky, conservative tan sweater and slacks she wore couldn't fully hide her womanly curves and long legs.

What had he gotten himself into? For a moment he was tempted to go back on his promise. But as always, he would remember those last hours with Thane, recall too easily Thane dying in a foreign land after fighting for his country, and Mike knew he had to keep his promise.

His only hope was that he wouldn't be spending too much time with Thane's widow.

Don't miss
EXPECTING A LONE STAR HEIR
by USA TODAY *bestselling author Sara Orwig,*
available November 2017 wherever
Harlequin® Desire books and ebooks are sold.

www.Harlequin.com

Want to give in to temptation with steamy tales of irresistible desire?

Check out **Harlequin® Presents®**, **Harlequin® Desire** and **Harlequin® Kimani™ Romance** books!

New books available every month!

CONNECT WITH US AT:

Harlequin.com/Community

 Facebook.com/HarlequinBooks

Twitter.com/HarlequinBooks

Instagram.com/HarlequinBooks

Pinterest.com/HarlequinBooks

ReaderService.com

H HARLEQUIN®

ROMANCE WHEN

PGENRE2017

Dear Reader,

I'm honored to help celebrate the 35th anniversary of Harlequin Desire. For many of those years, I was a secret Desire wannabe. I was writing for Harlequin Special Edition—a line I loved then and still love—but I also wanted desperately to write for Harlequin Desire. I loved the intense story lines, the tight focus on the romance, and the sparks between a man and a woman who were meant to be together. It wasn't all about passion in the sexual sense, but in the emotional sense, too. Strong feelings simmered so close to the surface that they threatened to singe a reader's fingers.

I was first published with Special Edition in 1992. It wasn't until 2006 that I published my first Harlequin Desire, with the Million Dollar Catch trilogy (*The Substitute Millionaire*, *The Unexpected Millionaire*, *The Ultimate Millionaire*). The pleasure I felt the first time I saw my name splashed across one of those gorgeous red covers stays with me today. The achievement of a fourteen-year dream.

Happy anniversary, Harlequin Desire, and thank you for thirty-five years of entertaining reads!

With love,

Susan Mallery

Author of the Happily Inc. romances

* * *

His voice came from right behind her.

At the open doorway, she turned and almost bumped into his chest.

"Oh, sorry." Wow, was his chest really that broad, or was she just so close it *looked* like he was taking up the whole world? Heat poured from his body, reaching for her, tingling her nerve endings. And he smelled so good, too.

Kelly shook her head and ignored the flutter of expectation awakening in the pit of her stomach. Deliberately, she fought for lighthearted, then tipped her head back and smiled up at him. "You know, I think I should get another point."

"For what?"

"For surprising you by not asking questions."

He studied her as if he were trying to figure out a puzzle. But after a second or two, he nodded. "You want to keep score? Then add this into the mix."

He pulled her in close and kissed her.